Henry Dryerre

Love idylls, ballads and other poems

Henry Dryerre

Love idylls, ballads and other poems

ISBN/EAN: 9783744723206

Printed in Europe, USA, Canada, Australia, Japan

Cover: Foto ©Andreas Hilbeck / pixelio.de

More available books at **www.hansebooks.com**

LOVE IDYLLS, BALLADS,

AND OTHER POEMS.

By HENRY DRYERRE.

BLAIRGOWRIE:
THE AUTHOR, 10 HIGH STREET.

EDINBURGH:
JOHN MENZIES & CO., HANOVER STREET.

1884.

PREFACE.

ApoLogy or explanation in some form or other is gene-
rally looked for on the appearance of a new volume,
particularly of poetry : I am afraid, however, unless the
volume itself can assert its own right to exist, the urgency
of friends and others whose judgment might be con-
sidered reliable will avail little as an excuse for publish-
ing. I am not confident I shall be justified for having
ventured to run the gauntlet of public criticism, but must
leave the matter in other hands now.

In the matter of arrangement, the reader will be good
enough to consider the classification, both throughout
the book, and in the contents pages, as only approximate ;
many of the pieces under one heading falling as readily
under some other.

My sincere thanks are hereby tendered the many kind
friends and subscribers who have interested themselves
in the production of this volume.

H. D.

BLAIRGOWRIE,
November, 1884.

CONTENTS.

—◦◦◦—

LOVE IDYLLS AND LYRICS.

BALLADS.

POEMS.

RONDELS AND SONNETS.

MISCELLANEOUS.

LOVE IDYLLS, BALLADS,

AND OTHER POEMS.

———○◦✠◦○———

AD POETAM. ✠

AWAKE, awake thou minstrel of the heart!
From depths of everlasting silence start,
And like yon star, shot from the heart of morn,
Prepare our night for glories yet unborn.
The dewy splendours of the rising sun
Are in our thoughts long ere the day's begun—
The eyeballs of the tear-dishevelled night
Are strainéd watching for the morning light.

Oh, sing of love! for love, for love we long—
Be it alone the burden of thy song;
Nor from thy quivering harp shall fall one strain
That is not echoed back to thee again.
Thy lips, more fine than ours, the thoughts may speak
For which in vain poor mortals utterance seek;
Thou, thou, divine, our fit expression be—
We have those thoughts we would express in thee!

Speak unto us of things we long to know,
And from thy heaven regard this earth below ;
Our hearts interpret thou, O radiant Face,
In whom our own lost lineaments we trace !
Are we of heaven that long of heaven to be ?
Canst say that aught is ours, birthright to thee ?
Are these our robes—these tattered thraldoms ?—say,
Thou whose meanest garment is the new-born day !

From out the curtained chambers of the morn,
With scattering song, step forth to hearts forlorn :
From dark recesses of the cavernous night
We cry aloud to thee for love, for light !
Speak purity to us who pine, impure,
Eternal things, where nought doth long endure ;
On starv'ling souls, unused to rich repast,
Some droppings from thy sumptuous table cast.

Increase our weeping for our finer joy,
For deeper peace, what peace we have, destroy ;
For surer balancing of tottering feet,
Some loftier height to climb, command, entreat.
What treasured joy is ours not got of tears ?
What faith, what hope, that owns not former fears ?
As night doth day, so surely doth our grief
Beget in us the only true relief.

O MANTI, all our yearnings are with thee,
Who singest not what is, but is to be ;
Our drooping eyesight with thy visions smite—
With thee alone of all the earth is sight !
Come forth, POIETA, from the gleamy mist
Where thou, divinely sphered, with brow morn-kiss'd,
Commun'st, adept, with things that have not been—
Create them for poor dwellers of the seen !

DREAM. ⁺

THERE is a mill I know,
  And down the stream
This flower will go,
  'As in a dream.
There is a maid who stands
  Beside the stream,
With claspéd hands,
  As in a dream.
Awake, my love : this flower
Will bring thee to the present hour.

I throw it on the stream,
  And standing cry :
As in a dream
  'Tis floating by.
And thou, my love, who stand'st
  Beside the stream,
With claspéd hands
  As in a dream,
This dreamy flower shall see,
And know my dreaming is of thee.

Dream, dream the mill I know,
  A dream the stream ;
This flower will go
  As in a dream :
A dreaming maiden stands
  Beside the stream—
I clasp my hands
  And dream I dream.
Haste, flower, and make her weep,
That we may struggle in our sleep.

⁺ Written one night, with "A Tear," p. 32,

KINNOULL.

KINNOULL, Kinnoull, thou height most dear,
Once more behold thy votary here !
On thy commanding brow I stand,
The monarch of a glorious land.
What richness greets my grateful eye,
What varied beauties 'neath me lie !
The Tay in silver silence softly flowing ;
The kine on verdant meadows distant lowing ;
Bold Mordune Top, in shaggy green,
The Lomonds in the distance seen ;
Sweet Orchard Neuk, secluded, still,
Old Abernethy 'neath the hill ;
Fair City, beaming in the sun,
Where many a valiant deed's been done—
Where many a theme, poetic, grand,
Doth still await the cunning hand ;
On emerald slopes, 'mid fertile fields,
A thousand nestling cottars' bields ;
Above, a heaven of dappled blue—
Beneath, an earth of summer hue :
Combine, my heart, these beauties rare,
No scene on all the earth can be more fair ;
Around, above, in distance, and at hand,
Behold ensample of the Scot's own land !
Oh, tell me not of warriors bold,
Whose deeds heroic are enrolled
On many an historic page,
For this and every future age :
That here they fought, and bled, and died,
Their country's safety and its pride ;
That here the poet sang his day,
And for fair Scotia tuned his lay.
No borrowed light is here required—
Behold the theme of bard inspired ! .

Behold such scene as nerved the heart
Of warrior stern to hold his part
'Gainst tyrant foes of Scotia's weal—
That nerved his heart, his hand, his steel !
The everlasting theme abides,
The beauty that all time derides ;
For us a land most fair of earth,
The land of Scotia and our birth—
A land, degenerate though we be,
Still nerves our heart to keep it free—
A land of beauty, love, and fame,
Oh, Scotia, Scotia, 'tis thy name !
Enthralling virtues float around,
We tread upon enhallowed ground :
Who, proudly owning home or birth
'Mid scenes like this, hath aught of worth
That doth not from his birthright spring—
A poet he, or warrior king ?
Is Scotia ours, that we care claim
Our fathers' virtues or their fame ?
     Stand firm, my heart, on thine own ground—
Thine eyes above, beneath, around,
In tearful gratitude but cast :
Thou hast the present—scorn the past !
While Scotia's noble mountains stand,
While scenes like these o'erspread the land,
While waving forests, rushing streams,
Refresh mine eyes and fill my dreams—
What deeds of fame or bardic lore
Can thee enhance whom I adore ?
Enough, thou treasured birthright given
To favoured race by gracious Heaven,
That Scots, by thy deep influence led,
Enraptured sang or freely bled—
Receiving through their native land
The workings of a higher hand.
     Kinnoull, Kinnoull ! I sigh farewell

To thy delights I love so well ;
Yet, everlasting joy remains
For him enlinked by memory's chains
To this fair scene beneath me spread,
These hills around, that sky o'erhead.
Endeared by nature's graces thou,
Yet more endeared by lover's vow ;
Two names within my heart are set,
Two names I never may forget :
One name is her's whose love is mine,
The other name, Kinnoull, is thine !

SHADOW.

A SHADOW falls upon the grass :
How strange that it should swiftly pass,
    Nor leave a trace behind :
The shadows of the heart
Have not so good a part,
    They are of other kind.

That shadow fell upon the grass,
As swift did fall, as swift did pass
    As any fleeting thought ;
But all our thought remains,
Remembering thoughtful pains,
    And yet, the thought is nought.

The shadows fall upon the grass,
And as they fall, so let them pass—
    To us it matters not :
Our life's a shadow all,
That swift as it doth fall,
    Doth fade, and is forgot.

BABY. †

BABY with the wondering eyes,
  Full of light, full of love,
Tell us where our heaven lies—
On the earth, or in the skies?
  Here, or there above?

Baby, baby, thou canst tell—
  Simple face, full of grace!
What we seek thou knowest well,
For, from heaven, where spirits dwell,
  Thou hast reached this place.

Baby with the silent eyes,
  Full of thought, uttering nought,
Thou art wiser than the wise—
There is more in thy surprise
  Than our earth hath taught.

Heaven's within thee, baby fair,
  Heaven is near—heaven is here;
For our search thou need'st not care—
Heaven thou bearest everywhere,
  Whether far or near.

And that look within thine eyes,
  Baby dear, stranger here,
Speaketh only thy surprise
We who seek forget the skies
  Whence we reached this sphere.

†. The coming of "Dora", my dear daughter,
is in April next.

⊹ BURNS.

THIS once forgive, O Bardic Shade,
Th' approach of one whose hand is made
For other work than polished lays
Of thoughtless flattery or praise.
Thy name, dear Burns, is in each heart,
And in our daily life takes part ;
It breathes around like common air,
And all are nourished by its care ;
Thy words, a ploughman thou of thought,
With such potential spirit fraught,
Have turned the soil of human hearts,
Till from each furrow daily starts
Such wealth of harvesting and flowers,
For winter dearth and summer hours,
That men, amazéd, grateful, sigh
To find what treasures in them lie.
Where'er we roam o'er Scotia dear
Thy genius and thy love appear :
The stars speak of thy tender love,
And earth doth answer heaven above ;
Each fragrant flower, each waving tree,
Each heath-clad hill and verdant lea ;
The wimpling burn and placid lake,
The warbling birds in bush and brake ;
The forms of nature loved by all,
Thy name aloud, emphatic, call !
New beauties spring where thou didst tread,
And all is blossom erstwhile dead ;
New meanings from things common start,
And finer feelings in each heart.
When tear-stained face and trembling tongue
Betray the heart with anguish wrung ;
When lovers meet in lonely dell,
The oft-told tale of love to tell ;

When brother Scots, where'er the land,
Stand face to face, firm hand in hand,
Or in the hell of sulphurous strife,
In fence of country and of life,
With knitted brow and flashing steel
Strike for their home and country's weal,—
Thy thoughts, potential, light each face,
And words superfluous give them place :
To tragic war, as peaceful arts,
Thy genius fire and grace imparts—
While Scots are brave, are true, are free,
As soon forget their land as thee !
    Yet, poet thou for every clime,
For every race, and for all time,
Shouldst thou, who lived and sang thy day
When few attended to thy lay,
On this poor earth one thought bestow,
And care, perchance, for aught below,—
Methinks, while men relieve their mind
For deeds unjust and thoughts unkind
Which thou didst suffer here on earth—
A man of tears, yet child of mirth—
Laudate anew thine honoured name,
And to thy credit place thy fame—
Methinks around those lips there may
A gentle smile of scorning play.
A poet thou, and care to claim
The credit of a poet's fame ?
Possessor thou of mines unwrought,
Creator of domains of thought,
Dispensing with a kingly hand
The heavenly gifts at thy command ;
And yet—and yet—one moment care,
Yea, for a single heart-throb, dare
To claim the virtue of that place
Which thou didst fill by Heaven's own grace ?
    No, no, dear Burns, forgive the **thought**,

'Twas thrust upon us all unsought ;
To such as thee, the kings of song,
To whom all earth and heaven belong,
There is no gift that mankind give
So sweet as simple leave to live ;
To be as thou wast as a voice
Which uttereth but another's choice—
Behind, unseen, unfelt by all,
Save he who hath the poet's call.
For there is certainly a soul
That doth the poet's soul control ;
He singeth at his own sweet will,
Subservient to a deeper still ;
The earth, the heavens, he grasps with might,
He readeth all men's thoughts aright ;
Within the garden of his heart
The blossoms of the future start,
And men who gather ripened fruit
Forget the poet was the root :—
Yet doth a still and secret hand
The poet's issues all command,
And all the thinkings of his heart
From depths unknown, unsounded, start :
Creator he, unwilled, unsought,
Created he, unknown, a thought.
Thou, Burns, thine own behests didst seek—
'Twas mortal that thou shouldst be weak ;
Yet, as we view thee, crowned with song,
What sympathies around thee throng !
The imperfections of our earth
Have faded at death's second birth :
Pedestalled on all time thou art,
True prophet of the human heart !

MY ROSE. +

I.

My rose, my rose!
  Its leaves are shaken,
To the winds it goes,
  Forgot, forsaken.
Dost seek that flower
  Whose odour fragrant
Through sunny hour
  Wooed zephyrs vagrant?

Quick! let us seize
  The petals flying
Adown the breeze,
  And save from dying!
With subtle art
  Our rose we'll fashion
To move the heart
  With tender passion.

II.

To the winds again
  Our rose we scatter—
Our work how vain
  With lifeless matter!
Yet is there still
  A fragrant being
In heart and will,
  With both agreeing.

And though our rose
  To the winds be shaken,
Its spirit grows,
  By form forsaken.
The seen, the near,
  Are gone for ever,—
Thou, rose, most dear,
  Canst perish never!

ⵜ. SELĒNĒ.

FAIR Moon, serenely calm and bright,
Afloat on sea of splendrous light,
Transforming, beautifying, grace,
Once more, my love, we're face to face—
Receive thy faithful lover, pray,
Who shuns the tinselled shows of day !
The nightingale doth sing to thee
Her sweetest, tenderest melody ;
The brook runs babbling on its way
That thou hast kissed it with thy ray ;
The dewdrops twinkle on the rose,
And up to heaven a fragrance goes
From every grateful flower that blows ;
The darkling trees, mysterious, sigh,
"Our Queen, Selēnē, floats the sky !"
Within the shadows of the trees
There glides the faintest, softest breeze—
A zephyr light, on wings of love,
That whispers low—"Look, look, above !
Our noble Queen is out to-night—
Look up, sweet flowers, behold the sight !"
The trembling grasses and the flowers,
The wakeful birds in fragrant bowers,
Where crowns of honeysuckle sweet
And climbing rose, embracing, meet,
With wondrous little creeping things
That gleam with dewy splendourings ;
A wandered bat, a beetle lone
That soothes my ear with drowsy drone ;
A thousand tiny insects' throats
That merrily add their chirping notes ;
From clover fields and meadows fine
The mellow lowing of the kine :—
All, all, dear Moon, are 'neath thy power,

And own the influence of this hour :
Devoted worshippers of thine,
Whose loving praise ascends with mine !
   Here, on this turfy bank reclining,
     I feed my greedy eyes on thee ;
   Forgot the daylight's heart-repining,
     And all the ills of life that be.
The poet's love, indeed, art thou !
Oh, when this wearied head shall bow
    Beneath the load of life,
    Refusing further strife
For sake of gain which is but loss,—
Come where the midnight breezes toss
The fallen leaves across my grave ;
For me, thy faithful lover, save
One tender, sympathetic ray,
'Twill recompense for life's dull day.
    As here, entranced, I lie,
    And listen to the sigh
Of tree to flower, and breeze to grass replying—
    I, too, I know not why,
    Sigh, sigh, responsive sigh—
Oh, sweeter than all life is this faint dying !
This glory floods my throbbing heart
  With thoughts expressionless and deep,
Vain certainties of life depart,
  And all is calm as dreamless sleep—
Day's cursèd certainties so fair,
That breed but doubt and dread despair ;
And here, within this realm of dreams,
A purer certainty there seems
Than aught that braggart day can show,
Or man who trusts in seeming, know.
  Selēnē ! hast thou nought to say
Against the babblings of the day ?
'Tis I, we hear ; 'tis thou, 'tis we,—
'Tis thus and thus in all we see :

'Tis plain—'tis true—'tis surely so :
No heaven above, or depth below,
No secret in this heart of ours,
But man, omnivorous, devours !
He knoweth all—the whence, the whither,
Our coming here, our going thither :
Across life's gilded stage he stalks,
Monopolist of words—and talks !
Hast thou no gift of words, dear Moon ?
Shouldst care exchange with blazing noon,
Who flashes on our dazéd sight,
With rush, and roar, and stunning might,
Disfiguring, crushing, and confusing,
Disdainful of all love and choosing,—
Relentless, pitiless, and stern—
Dost care, sweet Moon, such arts to learn ?

Forgive, my love ! I see thee smile
As thus I muse to thee the while.
Enough : I know thou dost resent
Words, words,—inane—incompetent,
And in thy smile the meaning's plain—
Wise silence speaks when words are vain.
Thou art a dream—a dreamer I—
That, grant me, for a certainty ;
And if a dreamer in the night
Doth dream he dreams, he dreams aright :
His truth is dream—his dream is true,
And here I dream I dream of you.
Oh, wake me not, intrusive day,
Ye sensibilities—away !
The moon, the stars, the trees, and I,
The flowers and grass whereon I lie—
Participants in love are we,
Disturb not our community !

Ha ! Phœbus rushes up the skies,

A debauchee, with flaming eyes ;
The stars, affrighted, faint away—
Beware, sweet Moon, the god of day !
He'll seize thee in his amorous arms,
And rifle thee of all thy charms :
Quick to yon cloud—retreat, retreat—
Adieu, my love—to-night we meet !

——⁂——

THE RILL, THE BROOK, THE STREAM, THE SEA.

TRICKLE, trickle, little rill,
From thy bed beneath the hill ;
Thou dost come from depths unknown,
With a purpose of thine own :
To the brook, the brook away,
For no trifling mortal stay.

Babble, babble, happy brook,
Never giving backward look
To the rill that gave thee rise—
Happy-careless, thoughtless-wise.
To the river haste away,
For no trifling mortal stay.

Murmur, murmur, noble stream,
'Tis the ocean is thy dream—
Ocean deep, and true, and free,
Waiting patiently for thee.
River, to thy love away,
For no trifling mortal stay.

Holy, calm, eternal sea !
Harmony and melody,
Depths unknown and frothy wave,
Continent and coral cave—
Yea, the heavens themselves are thine,
Clasp me in thine arms divine !

∴ THOU AND I.

WHEN thou and I
Fall out—good-bye!
  Without a doubt
That tear and sigh
  And scornful pout
Shall in the morning be forgot,
And longing fill each vacant thought.
  Inquirest why?
  'Tis thou and I!

For thou and I
May pale and sigh,
  And part in pain,
Yet, love will cry
  To meet again.
More, more than words, yea, thoughts are we,
Deeper than all we know and see
  Are thou and I
  Who say good-bye.

So, thou and I
May moan and sigh,
  And part in pain,
Nor know the why
  We kiss again :
We only know 'tis love, my dear,
And love is sweeter for each tear—
  Yea, for each sigh
  And sad good-bye.

Some passing cloud; tear memory.

⋅+⋅ TO THE LARK.

MOUNT, mount, with yonder lark, my heart,
    The spring is here, the jòyous spring ;
Thou, too, in Nature's song take part—
    Up with the merry lark and sing !

O lark, in heaven a speck, sing, sing !
    Would I might also cleave the sky,
And on a swift and quivering wing,
    To spheres of light and music fly !

Retard thy flight, sweet bird of song ;
    Forget not thou hast had thy birth,
With us below, who pine and long,
    Upon a dull and cheerless earth.

Is there a heaven within the blue,
    That thou on high the morn dost wait ?
And hast thou, then, a thinking, too,
    That thou, perchance, may reach its gate ?

'Tis surely so : that swelling song
    That floods the wavering morning air
Doth not to things of earth belong,
    Nor can with aught we know compare.

Sing, sing, thou bird celestial, sing !
    Of heavenly secrets thou dost know ;
From hidden springs of music bring
    Those draughts of song for us below.

And we who pine, and upward gaze,
    With claspéd hands and strainéd eyes,
Perchance shall join in grateful praise,
    Though earth be ours, and thine the skies :

Yea, thine the heavens, and ours the earth,
 The soaring thine, the longing ours ;
To thee the freedom of thy birth,
 With us the trammelling of our powers.

Yet heaven is ours, though heaven afar,
 And earth more distant daily seems :
As morning dims yon trembling star,
 Shall heaven eclipse earth's fairest dreams.

And with thy song, this happy morn,
 This morn of May, so fresh and fair,
Shall we, renewed, our grieving scorn,
 And shout our gladness on the air.

Mount, mount, with yonder lark, my heart,
 It is the spring, the joyous spring !
Thou, too, in Nature's song take part—
 Up with the merry lark, and sing !

SWEET BUNCH OF ROSES.

Sweet bunch of roses ! Maidens fair,
 Your fragrant gift a verse imposes
On its recipient : shall I dare,
  Sweet bunch of roses ?
I know not all each flower discloses,
 For thought extrinsic little care ;
But rose, to poet, e'er composes
 A theme that may with love compare.
This rondel, then, I pray, suppose is
 My thanks poetic for your rare
  Sweet bunch of roses.

MY FLOWERET FAIR.

MY floweret fair, you are so rare,
You are so rare—so rare and fair!
I cannot love you as I could,
Because you love not as I would:
   For love is love, and I love thee
    Truly, dearly, purely;
   And all I love must e'en love me,
    Truly, dearly, purely.

And if I love thee, love, and love
To hold thee far all else above,—
What say: Dost love me, simple sweet?
Dost think thy love for mine is meet?
    Dost love me dearly, purely?

By those fair brows, those tender eyes,
By those sweet lips, so rich a prize—
I know thy heart, so pure, so rare,
I know it well, and still I dare
    To love thee dearly, purely:

To love thee, love: for love can see
What is, and was, and is to be
In that we love; and I in thee
Behold thy love for future me,—
    Thy loving dearly, purely.

But love me, sweet, as I love thee:
'Tis now I love; now love thou me;
For love, though love, must cease to be
When those we love care not to see
    We love them dearly, purely.

STREAM.

STAY, marvel of our earth,
  A running stream—
Thou hast such constancy of mirth,
  Hast thou a dream?
Thou hast the sea at last,
  Hast aught behind?
Seek not to hurry past,
  Thou stream unkind.
There's that about thee that we love,
  And we who have our thought
Have deemed thee ofttimes far above
  Ourselves and all we've sought.
Thou hast a longing for the sea—
A longing for our sleep have we:
A song thou hast for all thy way—
We have but sighs, both night and day.

What, thus it is, indeed,
  Thou canst so sing—
Thou hast not in thee glistering bead
  But knows its spring.
Haste on, glad stream. Thy sea,
  With bosom wide,
Receptive, waits for thee:
  What can betide?
We have no joy like thine, thou stream,
  That singest hurrying past:
"Perchance——perchance——" is all our
    dream,
  We reach the sea at last.
But thou dost feel thy love is sure—
Thy birth, thou know'st, is heavenly pure:
We sigh, and pensive o'er thee dream—
O whence—whither—are we, stream?

QUESTIONINGS.

STAND still, my heart, and gaze around:
Where, in this universe, is found
The primal spring that being gives,
The life of all that breathes and lives?
Are we, who grasp the realms of space,
In turn enclasped in cold embrace
By visionary offspring of the brain—
Our own creations, yet in vain?
Whence this antagonism stern
'Twixt what we feel and what we learn—
This consciousness of better things
Than all our knowledge ever brings?—
This war incessant 'twixt the love
That nestles in the heart, and things above
The reachings of our trembling hands
That only mock our weak commands?
Return, my heart, return within!
Leave doubt, and all that men call sin
To those who seek from outward springs
The principles of deepest things.
I pass my hand across mine eyes,
And truth before, like crystal, lies.
The truth, indeed! Who is't conceives
The truth, and then its slave, believes
This laboured creature of his own
Commands, in strange familiar tone,
Obedience to some formal laws,
The laws that link effect with cause?
'Tis man, 'tis man—'tis longing man,
Whom angels from high heaven scan
With wondering gaze, to see him seek,
By devious paths and strivings weak,
To grasp the scintillations faint
That burst his earthly birth's restraint,

Or chase the fleeting gleams of heaven
From his own being sustenance given!

Knowledge seek'st thou? And who, I pray,
Is't seeks? Art not CONCEIVER? Say;
And is the knower, or the known,
The first in order of thine own?
Canst think infinities of thought
And not perceive the infinite brought
From depths eternal in thy heart,
Whence all thy thoughts, unbidden, start?
Canst think a hell, or blissful heaven,
Beyond conceptive powers given?
Or find'st thou in a single thought
One tittle more than thou hast brought?
What *is* thy thought or knowledge, then—
Creator, or create, of men?

Man, man! There comes a stirring time
When, all-forgetful of that clime
Of heavenly origin and grace
Whence spring the longings of our race,
Thou shalt behold, with strange surprise,
The image of thyself arise
From out fantastic forms of thought
Which thou so oft hadst weakly sought
In pleading tones, and sought in vain,
Nor knew thou didst the whole sustain!
We know not what we are, nor will;
Yet what we know is knowledge still,
And all we know is truly ours,
Created of creative powers:
Our consciousness, with widening rings,
From central *we* forever springs;
We know, we feel, but are, and are,
And ever are, from depths afar—
Eternal utterances we,

And more than all we know or see.
Knowledge? Avaunt, thou cumbering case
Of chrysalis life! thou hast thy place
With cast-off swathings of the mind—
We seek thy help? Behind, behind!
'Tis thus I scorn thee from my sight
To spheres of utterness and night,
And find within, and not abroad,
My own identity and God!

PARTING.

TEARS in thine eyes, my love,
   Sighs in the air,
Tender good-byes, my love,
   Hearts of despair!
From thee I go, my love,
   Ne'er to return—
Thinking forego, my love,
   While the hours burn!
Here, at thy feet, my love,
   Sigh I adieu,
Never to meet, my love,
   Tender and true!
Kiss me, my life, my love,
   Let thine arms twine—
To-morrow a wife, my love,
   Yet ever mine!

A TEAR.

I HAD a tear, my love. Last night,
        As on my couch I lay,
        I thought. "Perchance, at day,"
Thought I, "will come again the light."

That tear unbidden came: I know
        It not. Forbid the thought,
        My love, that thou art sought
By tears: they are but weak, I trow.

I wept; I cannot tell thee what.
        It seems as if our thought,
        Whate'er it be, is not
Within the one who has the thought.

I wept, I cried—"Oh, give me thought
        That is within my heart:"
        Perhaps, thought I, apart,
'Tis thou. Hast longed since last we sought?

'Tis strange, indeed, my love. It seems
        As if my thoughts in thee
        Were lost, and thou of me
Didst think, and both confused as dreams.

That tear I kept, I give thee now:
        'Twas it that, first concept
        Of longings deep, soft crept
Adown my cheek, nor knew its how.

For now I weep, nor know I why:
        Thy thought, my love, is me,
        Yet, since my thought is thee,
What thought hast thou? I sigh.

SLUMBER SONG.

Sleep, my babe, on mother's knee,
    Sleep, and do not fear;
Mother is a-watching thee,
    Father, too, is near.
Silver moon is in the sky,
    With her gaze so mild;
Mother sings her hush-a-bye—
    Sleep, my darling child.

All the birds have gone to rest
    Long and long ago;
And within your cosy nest
    You should sleep, you know.
Trees, and birds, and pretty flowers
    Fast asleep are they;
Moon and stars keep later hours,
    But they sleep by day.

Sleep, while o'er thee move the stars,
    With their eyes so bright—
Sleep, until through lattice-bars
    Streams morn's rosy light.
Sleep, and get the roses, too,
    Morn will bring to thee—
Sleep till drowsy eyes of blue
    Bright as stars shall be.

Sleepy, sleepy, drooping head,
    On a mother's breast,
Mother puts thee in thy bed,
    Birdie in its nest.
Sleep until the birdies wake,
    Till the east is red,
Mother never will forsake
    Baby in its bed.

DEPARTURE.

TURN, Bill, thy head away,
  The sun is in the west,
'Tis the last weary day,
  Before eternal rest.

Let Tom and little Nan
  Come in when all is o'er ;
And bear it like a man,
  Bill, like yourself, no more.

Dear heart, we've had our day
  Of happiness and peace,
And now I'm called away,
  'Twill be a sweet release.

It's been a weary time
  Since first I took to bed,
It's been an upward climb,
  I know, to get us bread.

I cannot help it, Bill—
  I'm glad I'm going away :
It's not been with my will
  I've had so long to stay.

Just kiss me dear, once more—
  You've been a good true man,
And when you see 'tis o'er,
  Be kind to Tom and Nan.

And if they ask for me
  When I am gone away—
Just say they'll come and see
  Me on some far-off day.

This much I know, dear Bill,
　There's nought in heaven for me
But ever, ever will
　Make me remember thee.

Remember thee, my dear,
　My girl and darling boy,
And wish that you were near
　To share in all my joy.

I'm wearied, Bill—no more ;
　Don't doubt, my dearest love,
There's happiness in store
　For those who love, above.

Kiss me again—again.
　'Twas a lovely day in May
When first you kissed me, Bill,
　And took my heart away.

A lovely day in spring,
　And everything so gay !
I hear the sky-lark sing
　As on that happy day.

Spring, spring for ever, dear,
　Will be our sweet delight—
Come near, my dear, come near,
　Kiss me—good night—good night !

A ROSE.

GIVE me that rose from out thy hair,
   In memory of this hour—
Not all the wealth of Indies fair
Can with this simple rose compare,
   Or with such gift endower.

Say, shall I kiss it, ere I place
   It carefully away?
Ah, love with tear-bedimméd face,
With flowing hair, and tender grace,
   Thy flower can ne'er decay.

The spirit of this fragrant rose
   Shall in my heart remain
When earth's faint phantasies and shows,
The dream of life, which comes and goes,
   Will go, nor come again.

Afar, afar, my feet may stray,
   But ne'er from thee, my heart:
'Tis little, love, to haste away—
'Tis nothing, love, to have to say,
   This night, this night, we part:

This night of sighs, farewells, and tears,
   Is in a glory set—
A glory that, in far-off years,
Shall chide us for our present fears,
   And joy anew beget.

Farewell! The rose-leaves scattering fall—
   To heaven a rose is given:
To rose or love, what can befall?
The scent and beauty of them all
   Live evermore in heaven.

CHANGED.

O DARLING mine! I think of thee,
  And know thy love is flown,
With tenderest idolatry
  I kneel before thy throne :
      Afar, afar,
      As yon bright star
Art thou removed from me—
  'Tis thine to shine in heaven above,
  'Tis mine to pine in silent love,
Content thy slave to be.

So near, my dear—so far away!
  I ponder o'er each word
Thou uttered'st on that happy day,
  When, like a nestling bird,
      Upon my breast
      Thou sank'st to rest,
Mine arms about thee thrown—
  Thine eyes were moist, thy lips were sweet,
  Our hearts were throbbing, beat for beat,
Thou called'st me thine own!

But now, but now, my darling one,
  Thou turn'st, estranged and cold—
Our morn has to the even run,
  To dross has changed our gold.
      The hours flit by,
      Afar I sigh,
Yet ever at thy side—
  O happiness for ever fled,
  O life, O love, for ever dead,
O heedless love, my bride!

ONE ONLY THEME.

ONE only theme my pen invites,
　　My willing heart enthralls ;
　One only hope my thoughts incites,
　　One joy alone ne'er palls :
Dost ask the theme, the hope, the joy?
'Tis love, 'tis love, without alloy !

　But shouldst thou seek to know the cause,
　　The wherefore of my choice ;
　Shouldst thou, inquiring, ask the laws
　　That regulate my joys—
I answer only, with a sigh,
I only love, but know not why.

　I love the dawn, the rising sun,
　　The lark, the scent of flowers ;
　I love the eve, when day is done,
　　And silent starlit hours—
I love them all—above, below,
Nor wherefore of my loving know.

　And thou, my love, the sum of all,
　　Around whom circling shine
　These minor joys, by nearness small,
　　Yet treasured joys of mine—
If so thou canst, explain to me
The wherefore of my loving thee !

　I know thy swift reply will come,
　　And find an utterance free,
　While I who love am only dumb,
　　And feel but mystery.
I hear thee say 'tis beauty—love—
That rules the earth and heaven above.

Yet, still my thoughts but outward flow,
    And sweetly rest on all ;
Nor do I seek the why to know,
    Or one faint thought recall :
I only know that all are dear,
The wherefore doth not yet appear.

Whithin my heart of hearts I feel
    A mystery abides
That earth and time may not reveal,
    Which all our thoughts derides :
The mystery of our being here
Is more than all our loving, dear.

Then, wherefore I of love should sing,
    And in my love rejoice,
Beseech me not an answering,
    Or question thou my choice :
Where'er I gaze 'tis love I see,
And love itself sufficeth me.

BEAUTY-POWER.

THE waving of that lady's hand
Doth such fine issues all command,
A thousand mobile hearts are blent
In one omnipotent intent :
A rushing spirit moves the world,
And mountains from their seat are hurled,
If she but spread those finger-tips,
Or deign to ope her queenly lips.

SIGH, MY LADY, SIGH AGAIN.

SIGH, my lady, sigh again,
Sweet the outcome of thy pain ;
Wouldst thou all that's lost regain ?—
    Sigh, my lady, sigh !

Happy swain, indeed, am I ;
Yet to that faint-heaving sigh
Fain would I with sigh reply ;—
    Sigh, my lady, sigh !

Smile and shadow o'er thy face
In succession swiftly race—
Tears, to tears, let smiles give place—
    Sigh, my lady, sigh !

Lift'st inquiring gaze to mine—
Canst thou not the thought divine ?
Ah, those eyes responsive shine—
    Sigh, my lady, sigh !

Yes, my love, our earthly bliss
May concentre in a kiss ;
Yet despite both this—and this—
    Sigh, my lady, sigh !

Earthly pleasures droop and die ;
All our longings upward fly—
Heaven is nearest those who sigh,
    Sigh, my lady, sigh !

ODE TO SPRING.

THE Spring, the Spring, the Spring has come,
  And earth is full of glee!
The air is flooded with the hum
  Of joyous harmony.

The lark mounts to the sky,
And from his vantage high
  Salutes the hasting morn,
Proclaiming, in glad song,
That she for whom all long
  Hath come to hearts forlorn.

The blackbirds in the brake
The evening echoes wake
  With pompous heralding,
While streams run merrily
To tell the smiling sea
  That Spring has come, sweet Spring!

The yellow primrose pale,
And cowslip, in the dale;
The busy humming bees
Round blossom-laden trees;
The river softly flowing
By cattle cheerful lowing;
The lambs, on daisied lea,
Frisking joyously;
The fragrant evening air,
And moon and stars so fair;
The silences of night,
With dawning of the light;
The tender, breathing soul
That pulsates through the whole;
The sweet, mysterious feeling
That o'er the heart comes stealing,—

Proclaim the approach of heavenly Spring,
To whom all hearts their homage bring !

Now unto us be kind, be gracious, Spring,
Who kneel before thee worshipping !
Thou seem'st of heavenly race, and we earth-born—
Beholding thee we feel our lot forlorn,
And all the longings of our heart we see
En-iris'd 'midst a mist of tears, in thee.
A wonder thou to this poor labouring earth,
For not of it, but heaven, hast thou thy birth :
The gaudy Summer may proceed from thee,
But who, O lovely Spring, hath gotten thee ?
Thine innocence proclaims thy heavenly birth,
Thine innocence which is so strange to earth—
A dream of heaven, a vision from afar,
As unattainable as yónder star.

O Spring, Spring, Spring !
  'Tis but mysterious sorrow
That prompts us now to sing,
  And joy from grief to borrow.

For now, when all is fair,
  And earth is fraught with gladness,
There comes that feeling rare,
  Of sweetest, tenderest sadness.

This blossom-scented air,
  These beauties bright and vernal,
Speak of a Spring more fair,
  The real, unseen, eternal.

Yet will we sing of thee,   .
  And sing in joyful measure ;
Whate'er our future be,
  Thou, Spring, art here, our treasure.

Take, then, take these advotive strains,
.That now ascend from woods and plains,
   And lark high-carolling,
With censer-offerings of the flowers—
Take what of praise our wakened powers
   Accord to thee, sweet Spring!

LADY, WITH THE JEWELLED HAND.

LADY, with the jewelled hand,
Thou hast more at thy command
   Than knight in armour clad :
Beckon thou but unto thee
Him thou wilt—on bended knee
   Behold thy servant glad !

Lady, with the lofty brow,
Thou hast fuller empire now
   Than queen upon her throne ;
From those temples, lily fair,
Breathes a spirit none may dare,
   And makes all wills thine own.

Lady, with the tender heart,
Thou hast still a better part
   Than she of temples fair :
Thou hast more at thy command
Than yon dame of jewelled hand
   And delicacies rare.

Lady, lady of my love !
Earth is more than heaven above
   If these be more than thou !
Dew to rosebud, wave to sea,
Are they all compared to thee,
   To thee I sing of now !

THE BARD AND HIS LYRE.

(Freely from Anacreon.)

ONE day I struck my trembling lyre,
　So long attuned to amorous lays ;
"Awake !" I cried, "and let each wire
　Proclaim a worthy hero's praise !
The deeds of Atreus' sons rehearse,
　To Cadmus give the honour due,
And while I chaunt in glowing verse,
　Do thou resound and throb anew !"

　　What !—" Love and only love,
　　All themes and powers above,
　　　　I sing !
　　Against thy will, I will,
　　To love celestial still
　　　　I cling !"

I changed my lyre in every part,
　The rebel strings renewed each one,
And with a bold but trembling heart
　Had brave Heraklēs' praise begun,—

　　When—" Love, and only love,
　　All themes and powers above,
　　　　I sing !
　　Restrain thy truant hand,
　　To themes of love command
　　　　Each string !"

Farewell, ye ancient heroes bold,
　Let other bards your praises sing,
My lyre, to deeds heroic cold,
　In praise of love shall ever ring !

THE ACTOR'S GRIEF.

" AN actor, Fred, you are, my boy,
    As good as ever seen ;
I saw the house in tears last night,
    All through that dying scene.

" That scene where 'tis your wife, you know,
    Who slips so quiet away ;
I tell you, pal, 'twas dreadful real
    To see you cry yon way.

" I saw the women, soft as babes,
    And men in box and pit
Were glad to turn their heads away,
    And blow their nose a bit.

" And, 'pon my word, behind the scenes,
    'Twas strange to see them cry—
You seemed to take it on so real,
    That wife of yours *did* die !

" 'Tis something strange to see you, Fred—
    How can you make the show ?
Just give a hint to help a pal,
    I'll keep it dark, you know."

The actor gazed with mournful eyes,
    A quiver on his lip,
And clasped his brother actor's hand
    In tender, nervous grip.

" Oh, never may you know it, Bill,
    Never the secret power
That makes it real to feign the grief
    That comes at death's dark hour !"

" Come, tell me, Fred—you needn't fear——"
    The actor turned away :

"My wife, dear Bill, that very hour,
    Was lying, lifeless clay.

"My darling, noble, struggling wife,
    My tender, loving mate!
God help the actor who must mock
    The agonies of fate!"

————o⚜o————

WERE ALL MY OWN.

WERE all my own which I have not,
    Who have but little worth—
A plenitude surpassing thought,
    And dwarfing heaven and earth:
All, all for love I'd freely give,
    And think the gift too small—
Were mine a thousand lives to live,
    One moment's love were all!

The vast eternities of space
    Are clustered in one spot;
The fruitage of this earthly race
    Concentres in one thought:
'Tis love that doth the spirit seem
    Of all we know and feel,
The real in this mazing dream,
    That self from self doth steal.

We sigh and long, we know not why,
    Our tears forever flow—
'Tis love that breathes in every sigh,
    We sigh for love, I know:
A sweetness mingles with our pain,
    That doth all pain surpass—
We tremble lest it come again,
    Yet hope it may not pass!

A SUMMER MORN.

ARISE, my love, and see the morning break,
　The lark in heaven is singing clear,
The woods from slumb'ring silence shivering wake,
　And all the earth is full of cheer.

From heart of dawn, as from an opening rose,
　A breeze blows sweetly o'er the lea ;
A fragrance, as from votive censer, goes
　Up to high heaven, from flower and tree.

From mead and grove, and far ethereal blue,
　Harmonious warblings greet mine ear :
Around, what rich profusion meets my view,
　Yet all how vain, till thou appear !

Come forth, my love ! come tripping o'er the plain,
　Thy cheeks aflush, as radiant as the morn—
Restore my inner consciousness again,
　Lost while I wander here forlorn.

Without thee, love, what all this beauteous scene,
　The sweetness of this summer air—
The dappled blue, the bright enamelled green,—
　What heaven or earth, howe'er so fair ?

A shimmering glory moves o'er Nature's face,
　A spirit fine stirs everywhere—
Within my heart, O wondrous Grace,
　O Spirit Beautiful, thou'rt there !

A whispering Presence floats upon the air—
　Interpreter, I feel thee now !
Art thou not she who layest all things bare ?
　O Spirit Beautiful, 'tis thou !

Have I not seen thee, tender, trembling sweet,
　On flowery banks, by running stream—

On sun-crowned hills beheld thee morning greet,
   And in the moonlight swiftly gleam ?

O Spirit Beautiful, divine ! To thee,
   For thee—with thee—'tis life to live !
Of thee, abiding consciousness give me—
   There is no deeper joy to give !

And, see, my love—she comes, she comes at last !
   Close to my heart I clasp thee, dear :
I gaze around—the dream, the dream is past,
   For thou, my love, the true, art here !

Thy calming hand upon my throbbing brow
   Do thou in silence soft impress :
O wondrous love, who near me stand'st, 'tis thou—
   'Tis thou alone dost all express !

Interpreter art thou to me of all—
   The earth, the heavens, but utter thee ;
The films of blindness from my vision fall
   When thou dost deign to smile on me.

Hark, yonder lark ! Thy hand in mine, my love ;
   What glory floods the morning sky !
O happy lark that float'st in heaven above,
   Thou surely hast thy sweetheart by !

Through shady grove, my love, by babbling stream,
   We'll wander on, this gladsome morn ;
They speak of thee, indeed—of thee, thou dream
   Of heaven to one, alas, earth-born.

And let me dream, so thou, my dream, remain—
   What sweet confusion fills my heart :
Ideal—real ? say not they are twain,
   Since thou consent'st we ne'er shall part !

"GONE."

GONE, with the dew upon her eyes,
    The morning dew ;
Gone, as we saw the sun arise,
And glory flame across the skies—
    Gone, gone, from mortal view !

A song of reapers filled the air,
    A happy song ;
And even while we smoothed her hair,
And hearts were hush'd in silent prayer,
    'Twas softly borne along.

    " Joy, joy, in the reaping
    Comforteth for weeping—
        Sowing is but sorrow ;
    Swing, swing, in measure,—
    See the golden treasure,
        Store it for the morrow !

    " Sing, sing, in gladness,
    Gone our tearful sadness,
        Harvest bright arriveth ;
    Where our secret weeping,
    Careful watchings keeping—
        Grieving that surviveth ?

    " Bind, bind, and gather !
    Oh, who careth rather
        For the dreary sowing?
    Heap, heap, our treasure,
    Sing in joyful measure,
        Home the wain is going !"

What could our hearts beseeching cry—
    Our breaking hearts?
Oh, as we raised our eyes on high,

And not with words, but sob and sigh,
    And tearful throbs and starts,

Pled trickling inward tears forlorn
    To God adored,
We felt the glory of the morn,
And, with the reapers of the corn,
    Were glad our corn was stored.

SUMMER'S REIGN.

SUMMER has her reign begun,
Swiftly mounts the morning sun,
Slowly, lingering, to his close,
Daily on his journey goes.
    Summer sun, with quickening ray,
    In our hearts hold summer sway!

From the heaven of cloudless blue,
Daily warmth and nightly dew,
Shed diffusive o'er the earth,
Make her laugh with summer mirth.
    Summer, summer, we would share
    In this gladness everywhere!

Evening comes, and from above
Moon and stars look down in love,
Down upon a world asleep,
While their silent guard they keep.
    Summer moon, with radiance calm,
    In our hearts drop heavenly balm!

Sun by day, and moon by night—
Heaven, thou art a beauteous sight!
Earth, thy heaven hath smiled on thee,
Liker heaven thou couldst not be!
    Summer, summer, here again,
    Ever in our hearts remain!

TWO RIVALS.

Two Muses woo my choice,
    Two fair ones press their suit ;
Sweet Poesy charms me with her voice,
    And Music, with her lute.

I stand between the two,
    And know not which to take—
The one I have no heart to woo,
    Lest th' other me forsake.

Without thee, Poesy fair,
    How wretched were my fate !
Who, loved by thee, can ever care
    With other muse to mate ?

Yet—Music, Music dear—
    What heavenly gifts are thine !
Didst thou forsake thy votary here,
    What recompense were mine !

'Tis thus I stand in doubt,
    Perplexed to please them both—
If they'd but woo me turn about,
    I'm sure I'd nothing loth ;

But when both Misses press
    Their earnest suit at once—
I really must, aside, confess
    To feeling like a dunce.

For then, perchance, polite,
    To this fair muse I pay
Some passing compliment, or write
    Some *vers de société ;*—

When sure as fate the other
    Will jealous look and sigh,

And all my efforts end in bother,
    Whichever way I try.

O Music, heavenly sweet!
    O Poesy, heavenly fair!
But let your hands, enclasping, meet,
    And your true lover share!

———◦◦◦——

STILL REMEMBER.

WHEN thou risest with the morn,
    And the mystery of the day,
Child of ebon night, new-born,
    Baptised with the dewy spray,
Greets thine eyes and senses fine,
Still remember thou art mine!

When the day is broad and calm,
    Phoebus ruling fierce and strong;
When the far-off evening's balm
    Seemeth all for which to long,—
When for darkness thou dost pine,
Still remember thou art mine!

Then, when comes the gentle eve,
    With her mellow, placid moon,
And the panting hearts that grieve
    'Neath the blazing orb of noon
Breathe an atmosphere divine,
Still remember thou art mine!

Still remember me in dreams,
    When thou sink'st to soft repose,
When the dreaming real seems,
    And the wish fulfilment knows—
When the heaven of love is thine,
Still remember thou art mine!

REMEMBRANCES.

GIVE me thy hand, my love,
　　And in sweet silence stand ;
The stars are twinkling far above,
　　And sleep is o'er the land.
And while men sleep and dream,
　　Forgetting fretful day,
Beside this ever-running stream
　　For one brief moment stay.

List to this self-same stream,
　　That runs so careless by !
To me, my love, that sound doth seem
　　A wondrous melody—
Awakening memories faint
　　And dreamy visions far—
Commingling heaven with earth's restraint,
　　As in its depths yon star.

Remembrance, mist, or dream—
　　Reflection from within :
What *are* those thoughts that twinkling gleam
　　Above life's clouding din ?
This eve so calm and still,
　　Those stars above so bright,
This happy, restless, singing rill—
　　Canst read them all aright ?

'Tis strange, my love, that I,
　　Who feel thee standing near,
And in the depths of thy fond eye
　　Behold myself appear,
Should pray thy gentle aid
　　To help my musings now ;
Yet, whither may I turn, dear maid ?
　　Interpreter art thou.

Thine eyes, so calm and still,
  Speak heaven within thy heart ;
At touch of those dear hands a thrill
  Of finer meanings start.
Art thou not of far heaven,
  Of heaven, our fatherland ?
Thou hast some sudden memory given
  To him who clasps thy hand !

O, earth, apparent—dream !
  O, heaven, a dream—the real !
From heart to heart love's lightnings gleam,
  And all in love reveal !
There is no heaven but love,
  And love hath ending not ;
Say—dwell we not in heaven above,
  And only here in thought ?

In thought, in thought, my dear,
  Thou stand'st beneath this sky ;
In thought thou see'st me standing near—
  In thought 'tis thou and I.
We live, and yet we dream ;
  We see, and yet are blind—
Forward, thou ever-running stream,
  What leavest thou behind ?

Perennial streams are we,
  From depths unknown we spring ;
'Tis from a past eternity
  These visions faint we bring.
Yet, dear, if love we know,
  Eternity is here ;
Love was, is now, and ever so,
  And hath not far or near.

While for a little space
  We walk this earth of ours,

With memories of our heavenly race,
  And unbegotten powers.
But as the morning dew
  On flower and tender grass,
So shall we swiftly pass from view—
  To heaven, our homeland, pass.

TO POESY.

O Poesy! Patient, gracious goddess thou,
  Invoked by all who seek the poet's fame,
  By some who barely know thy charming name—
By one, perchance, of that same genus now!
Howe'er, if thus it be, to fate I bow,
  Content if one faint spark, since not a flame,
  Of fire Promethean I from heaven may claim,
Nor dream of bays that deck the poet's brow.
Not for the wealth of all the fabulous East
  Would I exchange one favouring smile of thine,
Or leave to serve at god-Olympic feast,
  And press the nectarous grapes that make thy wine ;
And if, fair Poesy, 'tis not as thy priest,
  The lot of humble worshipper be mine !

OUR FATHERLAND.

Our Fatherland! Name dearer far
Than radiant sun or glittering star!
The ties that bind our hearts to thee
Are sweeter than all liberty;
Where'er our earthly lot be cast,
Our love and gratitude thou hast,
Afar, afar our feet may roam,
But thou art still our only home,
                Our Fatherland!

Our Fatherland! In dreams we see
The scenes of happy infancy—
In dreams we join the fireside throng,
And mingle in the dance and song;
Again we wander, fancy free,
O'er vale and hill, by stream and sea;
Again we feel 'tis sweet to live—
Thou only couldst such pleasures give,
                Our Fatherland!

Our Fatherland! The earth is fair
We wander o'er, and sweet the air;
The moon and stars look down at night
With tender sympathetic light;
The birds and flowers, the rivers' flow,
Are bright and beautiful, we know:
But oh, what longings in us burn!
From all, from all, to thee we turn,
                Our Fatherland!

SUPPLICATION.

My love, my life,
Forget me never,
Though wordless strife
Our lives may sever—
Though frozen lips
And finger tips
Be our sole speech henceforth forever!

Behind the mask
Of daily living,
Behind the task
Life's ever giving—
Behind it all,
Oh, hear me call,
Hear, love, in grace, and be forgiving!

Art thou not mine
By love's creation?
And canst divine
Some dearer station?
In vain, in vain!
'Twill thus remain—
Not we, but love, fixed our relation!

My love, my life,
Forget me never—
Let no vain strife
Our hearts e'er sever!
Return, return,
For thee I burn—
For thee, my love, my life, forever!

⊹ FAIR HELEN OF BALLINTIN-Y-GLOE.

'TIS midnight—weird and dismal noon,
The clouds rush o'er the spectre moon—
    There's moaning in the trees ;
A horseman rides with furious speed,
He urges on his foaming steed,
    Nor cloud nor moon he sees.

He nears the castle—'tis the gate :
What though the hour be weird and late ?
    He strikes with hand of mail :
"Ope, ope, within—the gates unbar !
I've ridden hard, I've ridden far,
    To tell a woeful tale !"

He strikes the gate—the warder cries,
"Who is the knight so late that hies
    To Drummond Castle gate ? "
"A messenger of fate am I,
From field of battle do I fly—
    Ope, ope, nor further prate ! "

The gates are opened wide, and in
The horseman rides with clanking din,
    His face is stern and pale :
"What meaneth all this revel rout,
These feasting sounds, that laughter shout,
    Which now my ears assail ?"

The warder scans the unvizored face—
But swifter than the lightning's race,
    The knight with mailéd hand
Has struck the warder to the ground !
"Die, slave, if thou dost utter sound
    Save at my own command !"

"My life, Sir John!" the warder cries—
"Thou hast it, slave—arise, arise,
  And speak in whispers low :
Is't so thy master weds to-night
Fair Helen of the tresses bright,
  Of Ballintin-y-gloe?

" I see it in thy face—be still !
For by the rood, this night my will
  Accomplishéd shall be !
If thou dost value life one jot,
My charger hold upon this spot—
  I may have need of thee."

With swift and silent steps he nears
The sounds of mirth that greet his ears,
  His hand is at his side :
He sees the guests within the hall,
He sees his Helen, queen of all,
  Sir Hilbert's promised bride !

"By Helen's brow, this night of glee
Shall prove a woeful night to thee,
  Sir Hilbert, trait'rous knave !
The power of right is in mine arm—
Protect, kind Heaven, protect from harm,
  The knight who comes to save !"

He thrusts the thronging serfs aside,
The doors he dashes open wide :
  A spectre of the night
Could not with deeper awe appal
Than he who stalks that ancient hall,
  In battle armour dight.

With stately mien and clanking tread,
Behold the spectre of the dead
  Move up the banquet-hall !
Fair Helen looks with startled eyes—

" My love, my love !" she faintly cries,
   And to the ground doth fall.

The master of the feast sits there,
With gaze entranced in dread despair
   Upon that figure grim ;
A fearful dew is on his brow,
He feels 'tis fate approaches now,
   The blazing lights grow dim.

" Stand forth, base knight !" the intruder cries,
" Behold, before thy wondering eyes,
   The friend whom thou didst slay !
If not in deed—the same, in thought,
By thee, with fiendish purpose sought,
   As on the field he lay.

" Sir Hilbert, thou wert all my friend—
'Twere curséd leniency to fend
   Such treachery as thine ;
Thou, cousin once, but now my foe,
Shalt fulness of my vengeance know
   Ere thou hast quaffed thy wine !

" *Thou* would'st, indeed, my Helen wed,
And prate of me as of the dead—
   The dead, indeed, for thee !
Thou covet these brave walls of mine,
The heirdom of a noble line
   Of warrior ancestry !

" Reach down thy sword, thine armour don—
Thou'lt surely need it ere the dawn
   Doth gild the eastern tower !
'Tis thou or I, thou treacherous friend,
Must bite the dust, and God forfend
   The righteous in this hour ! "

Quick to the courtyard speed they all,
With flashing torches from the hall,

To light the battle fray ;
Their swords are drawn, they forward spring,
On casque and helm they clash and ring—
    'Tis conquer he who may !

They strike and ward—advance, retire,
While round them flashes circling fire,
    And shoutings rend the sky :
"Thou hast it, John !—take that, thou curse !"
"I'll pay, Sir Hilbert, with a worse !"
    'Tis thus they fighting cry.

The thronging host, with torches bright,
Shout now the one, the other, knight,
    All eager for the fray ;
Fair Helen at her window stands,
With strainéd eyes and claspéd hands,
    And for her love doth pray.

A feint Sir John makes at his foe—
Sir Hilbert wards—his sword is low—
    Sir John his time doth see ;
His blade is flashing in the air—
"Sir John, Sir John, thy kinsman spare !
    'Tis Helen cries to thee !"

What need to cry his Helen's voice
Doth now command his wavering choice ?
    To hear is to obey :
His arm's arrested in the air—
His cousin still he'll pardon, spare,
    Though power is his to slay.

One wavering second doth he stand,
With sword upraiséd in his hand—
    One second swiftly flown !
Sir Hilbert strikes, nor strikes in vain,
There is a cry, a cry of pain—
    "Sir John, Sir John is down !"

But swifter than the arrow's flight,
Sir John hath raised his form of might,
    And on his foeman springs ;
His sword is gone, his head is bare,
One daggered hand is in the air,
    The other, helpless, swings.

That dagger is in feeble grasp!
Fair Helen doth her bosom clasp—
    Alas, the wrong is right!
His foeman strikes with vengeful hand—
Sir John lies bleeding on the strand,
    A sad and woeful sight.

"Down with Sir Hilbert!" is the cry
That now resoundeth to the sky—
    "A noble knight is slain!
Down with the cur who could betray
A knight so brave in battle fray
    As from his blow refrain!"

Swift to the gate Sir Hilbert hies,
And warder with the charger spies—
    He seizes it to start :
The warder knoweth not 'tis he,
Cries, "Blow for blow I give to thee!"
    And stabs him to the heart!

Within the hall Sir John is laid,
His wounds are dressed, and hand and head
    Are kissed by Helen fair ;
"Thou'lt live, my love," she gently sighs,
While tender tears bedim her eyes—
    "Thou didst thy kinsman spare."

He smiled, and kissed her jewelled hand :
"My lady love, 'tis thy command,
    No other law I know."
He lived, and happy were the pair,
Sir John the brave and Helen fair
    Of Ballintin-y-gloe.

WHAT TREASURES OF OUR HEARTS HAVE WE?

A SONG FOR CHRISTMAS MORN.

WHAT treasures of our hearts have we,
O Jesu fair, to give to Thee,
 This joyful Christmas morn?
Our hearts are love, our voice is song—
Our hearts, our voice, to Thee belong:
Oh, deign receive what Thou hast given,
Thou Love, Thou Joy of earth and heaven!
   Hail, hail, bright Christmas morn!

We know not all Thou didst forsake
When Thou Thy home on earth didst make,
 That wondrous Christmas morn:
What splendours of Thy heavenly seat
Didst Thou renounce, this earth to greet—
What heavenly joys Thyself deny,
To live, to toil, to weep, to die!
   Hail, hail, sweet Christmas morn!

Our feeble words, our trembling voice,
Refuse the utterance of our choice,
 This joyful Christmas morn;
Our hearts, our hands, to Thee we raise—
Oh, help us in our stammering praise;
Let song resound in heaven and earth—
It is the morning of Thy birth!
   Hail, hail, glad Christmas morn!

*I wrote this and " O the Idcully" (p. 150) one
night many years ago — in great despondency.
not 4 work, alone, estrangement between my,*

FRATER NOSTER.

JESUS ! all our hopes and sorrows
    We may utter unto Thee,
Trembling faith from knowledge borrows
    Comfort in our misery.
Thou, we know, didst pine and languish,
    That Thou might'st our freedom bring,
Suffer cruellest pain and anguish
    For our surest comforting !

Jesus ! Thou alone dost know us,
    Thou alone our griefs canst feel ;
Over us, and firm below us
    Daily love Thou dost reveal.
Tender are Thy mercies ever,
    Fitful is our love to Thee,
Yet we know Thou never, never,
    Wilt forsake Thy family.

Jesus ! brethren Thou didst call us,
    When Thou deigned'st to walk this earth,
Oh, let nothing e'er appal us,
    Nothing hide from us our birth !
Brother, hear ! let nought betide us,
    While as pilgrims here we roam,
Through this life Thou lived'st, guide us,
    Onward, upward, to our home !

LITTLE WILLIE'S VISION.

OH, mother, I hear the angels sing,
   As in my bed I lie,
And see such millions clustering
   Up in the golden sky !
And all the night they come and go,
   And beckon me away :
" Dear Willie, leave that earth, below,
   And come up here," they say.

What shall I do, dear mother, tell ?
   'Tis every night the same,
And though I love you all so well,
   They call my very name.
And, strange, dear mother, that it seems
   I know each one up there,
And everything within my dreams
   Is real as anywhere !

Oh, what a sound and glorious sight
   To hear and see them all
Come rushing down the silent night,
   And on your Willie call !
Some night, dear mother, I must go—
   How can I here remain
When such a host invite me so
   To join their shining train ?

And one bright angel o'er the rest
   Holds out his hands to me,
And sometimes lifts me to his breast,
   To kiss me tenderly.
Then all the angels shout for joy
   And wave their glistening wings—
But, kiss me, mother, kiss your boy,
   And see what morning brings.

*   *   *   *   *

The morning came, all fresh and fair,
   The lark sang in the sky,
The mother smoothed her darling's hair,
   With many a sob and sigh.
Up in the blue her Willie sings,
   In accents loud and clear—
" Not long, dear mother, ere bright wings
   Shall bear you, too, up here ! "

LONGINGS.

O FOR rest, for peacefulness, and ease !
  Not greedy of thy gifts, O fortune, I,
Yet, as I stretch my limbs beneath these trees,
  And gaze into the depths of summer sky,
     My heart is set a-longing,
      Swift thoughts and hopes come thronging,
   And in the midst of summer joy, I sigh.

Thou human heart ! so oft, so oft beset
  With thoughts like these, when all is calm and fair ;
This summer beauty only doth beget
  Within our hearts a deeper love and care.
     While birds are sweetly singing,
      Our thoughts afar are winging
   To heaven, whence springs this beauty everywhere.

'Tis thus we long, 'tis thus we pine and sigh,
  For something deeper than the all we see,
Yet have this faith, though life doth quickly fly,
  And with our life our longings cease to be.
     This faith, this intuition—
      In heaven a sweet fruition
   Of all our hopes and longings find shall we.

DOLCE FAR NIENTE.

HIST! some one comes this way—
　It is my love, I know it!
Oh, who, on summer day,
Among the scented hay,
With her he loves not far away,
　Can help his being poet?

Although no poet I,
　Yet, comes a little thinking;
And when my love is by,
And from her laughing eye,
The gleaming shafts of Cupid fly,
　The thoughts and words come clinking.

I see love in each flower,
　In cloud, and sun-kissed river;
'Tis present every hour,
In sunshine and in shower,—
'Tis everywhere the moving power,
　And shall be so forever.

List to yon thrush's lay,
　That o'er the mead comes swelling:
Not to the god of day
Doth he devotions pay,
But to his mate on blossomed spray
　His throbbing love he's telling.

I gaze into the blue,
　As here, at ease, I'm lying;
The sky, like lover true,
All-amorous stoops to view
Earth's lovely face of summer hue,
　That blushes her replying.

A soft breeze stirs my hair,
  Sweet fragrance loads my senses,
A love-song fills the air
That doth my longings share,
'Tis love and beauty everywhere,
  In all their moods and tenses!

Ha, here my dear, at last,
  To cheer thy lover lonely!
Come,—witching power thou hast:
Together let's forecast
A future that will dim the past,
  If but in dreaming only!

DOUBTING.

THERE is a love that hath no speech,
  No speech save smiles and tears;
Oh, say not I thy heart must teach
  To quell its trembling fears!
Within my heart I hold but one—
  One love alone I prize;
But words, indeed, I ever shun,
  To enhance me in thine eyes.
I love thee, love; look in mine eyes,
  This hand enclasp with thine;
I ask thee not to speak thy love,
  Then wherefore should I mine?
The sky is bright, the earth is fair—
Thy lips to mine—away all care!

MERRY MERRY LOVE.

THE violets come with Spring,
  With Summer come the roses,
And Autumn's golden harvesting
  The wealth of earth discloses.
Then cometh Winter's frost,
  Heigho ! the winds are wailing !
The spectre-trees are tempest toss'd,
  And Nature all is ailing.

      But love, my merry merry love,
        Remains with me forever,
      There's nought below and nought above
        Can our two spirits sever !

Quick, lark, to yonder heaven,
  On joyful wing ascending—
My heart a song to heaven hath given
  With theme, like thine, unending,
Eternal love we sing,
  Yet sing we not together ;
Thou carollest blithely in the spring,
  But how in winter weather?

      Yet love, my merry merry love,
        Remains with me forever,
      There's nought below and nought above
        Can our two spirits sever !

The swallows come and go,
  The brook flows to the river,
The river to the sea doth flow,
  And thus with all forever.
Forever swift decay,
  Forever change and sorrow,
What we, perchance, enjoy to-day

> But love, my merry merry love,
>   Remains with me forever,
> There's nought below and nought above
>   Can our two spirits sever !

THE POET'S LANGUAGE.

I.

NOT all the tender greenery of spring,
  Or lush luxuriousness of summer time,
With fluttering, happy birds, on freedom's wing,
  Are more than symbols for the Poet's rhyme :
There is a longing in his heart that is beyond his
    choice,
Earth may suggest its meaning, but is not his voice.

II.

Quick, grasp the subtle beauties of the earth,
  With fingers heavenly-delicate and fine,
And weave a garment worthy of thy birth,
  O Poet stranger, from the realms divine !
'Tis thou alone canst utter what we may but feel,
Thou only, through things common, canst celestial
    things reveal.

III.

In vain !   Not here shalt thou e'er fitly speak
  The thronging visions of thy trancéd soul,
And all our pleadings only shew how weak
  The hearts that would thy utterance pure control :
There is a mystery, we know, we feel, in thee,
That never on this earth shall find an utterance free.

TURLUM.

GIN ye ha'e thochts o' warldly care,
  An' fain wad hint ye birl them,
Juist tak' a waucht o' caller air,
  An' stap awa' to Turlum !
      To Turlum tap, hurrah, hurrah !
      Through briery bush and birken shaw
      We'll warsel bauldly till we craw
        Upo' the tap o' Turlum !

It's a' oor ain, the lan' we see,
  Oor lips at lairds we curl them ;
Feint ane has mair o' richt than we,
  Wha speil the heichts o' Turlum !
      To Turlum tap, hurrah, hurrah !
      The lairds had better bide awa',
      Or aiblins they may get a fa'
        As heich's the tap o' Turlum !

There's Sandy wi' the pawky mou',
  My faith an' he could dirl them !
An' Jock, an' Hal, though douce the noo,
  Micht len' a han' on Turlum !
      To Turlum tap, hurrah, hurrah !
      Gin we the lairds should meet ava,
      Let's houp they'll no begin to craw
        Upo' the heichts o' Turlum !

Hurrah, my lads, the tap at last !
  Oor throats wi' will we'll dirl them,
The triumph's oors, the labour's past,
  We've struck the heichts o' Turlum.
      Hurrah, hurrah, for Turlum tap !
      For on the tap there is a cap,
      An' in that cap there is a drap—
        Here's to ye, bauld auld Turlum !

An' here's to Scotland's hills and plains,
  While bonnets heich we birl them ;
The Scottish bluid loups in oor veins
  Upo' the heichts o' Turlum !
    For Turlum, lads, hip, hip, hurrah !
    An' sweet Strathearn, the pride o' a' !
    We're Scotia's sons, an' weel may blaw
      Upo' the heichts o' Turlum !

Again we'll make the welkin ring,
  As Scotia's sangs we skirl them,
An' may we never dowfier sing
  Than noo we sing on Turlum !
    Hurrah, for Turlum tap, hurrah !
    Aince mair, hurrah ! an' then awa'—
    We'll ne'er forget this day ower a'
      Upo' the heichts o' Turlum !

ONE WISH.

I WOULD that I could write
  One perfect thought,
As heavenly pure, as bright
  As jewel wrought .
From grand Golconda's secret mine,
Upon some maiden's breast to shine.

  Or, as a dewdrop fair
    Upon a rose
  That on the morning air
    Her perfume throws :
A microsphere of heaven above,
In nectarous depths of fragrant love.

A SONG OF SEVERED LOVE.

You are not distant, dear,
  Though many a mile away,
They know not either far or near
  Who live beneath love's sway :
Yet oh, my dear, tho' love should smile at space,
I weary day and night to see thy face.

To see thy face, my dear,
  To touch thy lips once more,
To hear thee whisper in my ear
  The words oft heard before ;
To feel thy darling head upon my breast,
And hear thee say again thou loved'st me best.

O never more, my dear,
  Will come again the past ;
We wondered oft, e'en while 'twas here,
  Such peace so long could last.
We kissed and smiled, but silent and in fear :
" We love too well," you said, " too well, my dear."

Then, better love too well
  Than never love at all ;
They only love whose love can tell
  Of triumph and of fall ;
And they who once have tasted perfect bliss
Are thence exempt from utter wretchedness.

And shall we weep then, dear,
  For our departed bliss ?
Doth love delight no other sphere,
  And only smile on this ?
Dry, dry thine eyes, and put away all fear—
'Twill come again, dear love, tho' never here.

The breath of flowers, my dear,
   Goes up, sweet flowers, to heaven ;
Heart longings, deep and voiceless here,
   Are there full utterance given.
So, all the scent and glory of the past
Live evermore, as we shall know at last.

We will not weep, then, dear,
   Ev'n tho' our hearts grow cold,
Ev'n tho' dear earth no more appear
   God-lovely as of old ;
The beauty darkened here lives glorious above,
And heaven hath every loveliness for them who love.

DESPERANS.

THE rain is pattering 'mong the leaves,
   The clouds hang low and still,
The birds are twittering 'neath the eaves,
   A mist rests on the hill ;
A brooding stillness loads the air,
And in my heart is dull despair.

A dull despair, a trembling thought
   That all I see but seems,
That all this seeming real is nought
   But phantasies and dreams :
That all I am and all I see
Are not what is, but is to be.

What is to be ? What was it not,
   What is, as far away,—
What is to be is but a thought,
   Retreating day by day :
A shadow stalks our steps before,
And with our haste but hastes the more.

A throbbing fullness of the heart,
  A fervency of brain,
A mind that would with all take part,
  A heart concept of pain—
These are the dowries of our birth,
The heirdom of our place on earth.

O sweetening raindrops, busy eaves,
  O clouds, so low and still,
O gurgling brooklet, quivering leaves,
  O mist on vale and hill—
Ye all in Nature's plan have part,
What lot is ours, inform our heart!

In struggling incompleteness now,
  Dissatisfied, content,
Expanding heart, contracting brow,
  With tearful study spent—
Behold, how feeble mortals speak,
From earth and sky instruction seek.

In vain I gaze around—in vain :
  There comes no thought to soothe,
No hand to calm this questioning pain,
  This careful forehead smoothe—
The dulness of this dead despair
Is more than all the earth and air.

Forgive, forget the human cry
  That sought your aid—in vain—
Ye are but silent dreams, and I,
  And I, a dream of pain,
Despairing, hope the dream may break,
And to my life in death awake!

—o—

DRUMMOND GARDENS.

WHILE other themes of lesser worth,
And other scenes on this fair earth
   Find fitting praise in song,
For ever shall remain unsung
The praise that floods our faltering tongue,
   The thoughts that climb and long,

As 'midst thy beauties, Drummond fair,
We revel in the odorous air
   This happy summer day ;
Oh, had we power to clothe in sound
The thoughts within, by weakness bound,
   Thou hadst a noble lay !

Our eyes are filled with longing tears,
Where'er we gaze a mist appears,
   A tender mist from heaven ;
Receive the offerings of our heart—
These tears that now unbidden start—
   To us sole utterance given.

And, should afar our lot be cast,
And this sweet day with thee be last,
   Amen ! let fate decree ;
We leave thee, beauteous scene, in peace,
But never can our souls release
   The thoughts we have of thee !

NAY, NAY, MY LOVE.

NAY, nay, my love, thou knowest not :
True hearts are ne'er by grief forgot,
And love, if love, is all a cry,
" Oh, let me love, or let me die ! "

The rose may fade upon thy cheek,
And silver these fair tresses streak—
The dew-drop glisten in thine eye,
And all thy hopes and feelings die ;

Yet will there one desire remain,
One tearful bliss, one blissful pain—
Thy throbbing heart still find one cry,
" Oh, let me love, or let me die ! "

I know it, love, I know it well,
Too truly, love, its truth can tell :
With weak performance, strong desire,
External calm, internal fire—

Thy lover knoweth all the grief,
The sinking heart, the slow relief,
The import full of that strange cry,
"Oh, let me love, or let me die ! "

 Credo.

O NIGHT, NIGHT.

O Night, Night, so silent, calm, and deep,
Within thy heart what secrets dost thou keep!
    Wilt utter them to me?
The flaunting day—the trifling, vacant day,
Doth seek to steal my love from thee away,
    Yet am I true to thee.
      Ah me, reproachful Night,
      How sad is mortals' plight,
That ever thus our loves enthralled must be!
      Thou knowest I am thine,
      Yet daily I must pine
For that communion dear but found with thee.

O Night, Night, so heavenly-pure and sweet—
Of thy all-bounteous grace my needings meet!
    Thou knowest I am weak:
Within, without, what longings seek mine aid—
How much on weakest mortal here is stayed!
    Where shall I helping seek?
      I live for those I love,
      Nor have I thought above
The thoughtful wish of those whose love is mine;
      Yet all my hopes are vain—
      Renew my heart again—
Uphold me till I need no help of thine!

O Night, Night, thy kindly watchings keep,
While I, a-wearied, stretch myself in sleep—
    I plead thy gentle aid;
With wavering will and all too-trivial might
I struggle day by day to do the right,
    Nor know on what I'm stayed—
      Believing still that all
      Aright shall somehow fall,

That all is right and good though nought is known.
Thus, thus, my loving Night,
I trust thee till the light,
And cry to thee, yet know not all my moan.

ONCE.

ONCE, Marian, thou didst love,
  Once fondly thought of me,
And by yon heaven above
  I loved thee faithfully !
Now, thou canst scorn a heart
  That would have bled for thee,
Canst slight the tears that start
  To plead my love for thee.

Go, darling, go and wed
  Where thou thy heart hast set,
And may that love now dead
  Ne'er rise reproachful yet.
Once, once indeed, didst thou
  To love responsive sigh,
And though thou turnest now,
  True love can never die.

To memories of past days
  Thou'lt yet regretful turn,
And through a tearful haze
  Feel love within thee burn.
Heaven grant thee strength to bear
  The anguish of that hour,
When none thy grief may share,
  Or ease its bitter power !

SPRINGTIME.

X (Written in the City, 1870.) +

O SPRINGTIME, dear Springtime, thou'rt here again,
    I know,
The hills are robed in green again, in flowers the
    plains below ;
The trees clap hands of joyfulness, and wave their
    pennons gay,
And little birds in shady nooks sing welcomes all the
    day ;
All Nature's glad and beautiful—above, around,
    below—
Thou'rt here again, dear Springtime—thou'rt here
    again, I know.

O Springtime, dear Springtime, thou'rt here again, I
    know,
And Springtime, dear Springtime, I always loved thee
    so !
Yet weariness and heaviness are with me all the day,
As in my heart I fancy thy dear beauties far away,
Again, with all thy treasures, thou art here again, I
    know,
And morn till eve with longing heart my weary way I
    go.

O primrose and cowslip, adown yon shady dell,
O mossy stones, and waving grass, and ferns I love so
    well ;
O hedges white with hawthorn bloom, O perfume ,
    faint and sweet,
O silent woods and lonely lanes, where happy lovers
    meet ;
O winding stream, forever gay, and singing as you
    go—

How ye all look and feel this day, with aching heart
    I know.

When shall I wander on again as once in days gone
    by,
And " I thank Thee, Father, that I live," again be my
    glad cry !
It is not life to live up here, amidst the shows of things—
If life be such, then let me die, and live the life death
    brings.
O Springtime, dear Springtime !—I make one only
    cry,—
If I might only see thee once, and her, before I die !

Heaven's curses on the brutal crowd, with callous
  .   hearts and cold,
Who trample every beauty down to grasp their much-
    loved gold !
Each day my heart is smitten as their greedy eyes I
    meet,
With fear they next may turn thy way, with desecrating
    feet.
O Springtime, dear Springtime—I long both night
    and day,
Yet 'tis not all regret I feel to know thou'rt far away.

Adieu, thou tender Springtime—I bid thee sad adieu,
And brace a nerveless heart to strive and struggle on
    on anew,
May Heaven forgive the wayward heart that hath no
    part with hand—
I'll think no more till Springtime come within the
    Better Land ;
O Springtime, dear Springtime, thou'rt here again, I
    know,
But all the beauty lives above thou shadowest forth
    below.

—◦✄◦—

✢. THE MINSTREL TO HIS LOVE.

To her I love, so dearly love,
   I sing and play all day,
Nor will I listen to one word
   Of all she has to say.
I sit and sing and play—
   How swift the summer flies!
My song goes right into her heart,
   And shineth from her eyes.

To that dear one, my love alone,
   I never give one glance:
I know to seem in thought afar,
   Our nearness doth enhance.
"When shall our wedding day
   Come fluttering down the sky?"
I hear her whispering in my ear,
   But know not she is by.

To her, to her, my treasure dear,
   My heart in throbs goes out,
Yet would I not for anything
   Relieve her of one doubt.
I sit and sing and play—
   How swift the summer flies!
And all the thinkings of my song
   Shine out from her dear eyes.

I touch my dear love's lips with mine,
   And whisper, bending low,
"What thought of mine hast thou not got,
   What pleasure that I know?
How can I dearer be,
   When wed, than now I kiss?
What happier love will then be ours
   Than this—and this—and this?"

But all how vain to plead with her!
  Words, words avail me nought :
"When shall our wedding be, my love?"
  Her daily, nightly thought.
When shall it be? Tra-la!
  I'll sing and play all day—
Mine eyes are fixed on yonder cloud,
  And thou art far away!

But swift the summer flies, I trow,
  And vainly must I sing
While all her thoughts are circling round
  A simple wedding ring.
"When shall it be?" she sighs—
  Ah, who can sigh so well!
So, ere the roses fade, my love,
  We'll hear the marriage bell!

SIMILITUDE.

HERE, while through life we swiftly pass,
Each heart's a photographic glass;
On sensitivities of mind
Faint images are left behind,
But only in the favouring night
Come forth the beauties of the light,
And in the darkest, saddest hour,
The brightest memories show their power.

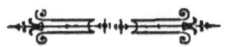

COME NEAR ME.

COME near me, dear, come near me, dear,
　　I have not long to stay,
And put your hand in mine, my dear,
　　In your old way.
A little while the sun will set,
　　And darkness fill the land,
A little and I'll feel no more
　　Thy dear, dear hand.
Though I have sorrowed many a day,
　　Love pays for all, and more,
And don't you weep for what, my dear,
　　　　Is nearly o'er,
　　　　Thank God, is nearly o'er.

Bend down a little closer, dear,
　　And raise my head :—just so ;
Before another hour, my dear,
　　It will lie low.
And put your hand upon my brow,
　　'Tis thus I'd like to die—
I said I could not go, my dear,
　　And you not by.
You'll stay a little while, my dear?—
　　Bend lower still, still lower,
And don't you weep for what, my dear,
　　　　Is nearly o'er,
　　　　Thank God, is nearly o'er.

Dear, how I've loved you all along,
　　Through evil times and good,
Since when we spoke and kissed our last
　　Down in the wood.
Those angry words—those angry words—
　　Why did you heed them, dear?

One little kiss before I go,—
　He need not fear.
He need not fear, though love is love,
　And love for evermore ;
But don't you weep for what, my love,
　　Is nearly o'er,
　　Thank God, is nearly o'er.

The shadows lengthen on the wall :
　O weary heart and weak !
Let me lie down to rest, my dear,
　I cannot speak.
There's a withered rose beneath my head,
　A tress of hair you know—
I wish thou'dst kiss me once again,
　For long ago.
I cannot see—where are you, dear ?
　The sun is surely set ;
How dark and cold ! Come near me, dear,
　The dew is wet.
There's a withered rose and a lock of hair,
　And the happy ring you wore ;
And don't you weep for what, my dear,
　　Is nearly o'er,
　　Thank God, is o'er, is o'er.

matter, regarding which he knew
in his letter, however, he said that we
did know was a poem beginning
"Come near me, dear. Come near me, I

DREAMY JEAMIE.

Jeamie, Jeamie, darling Jeamie!
Distant-gazing, wistful, dreamy,
Does your pa use heavy hand,
When you shirk his stern command?
Is he cruel to his boy
Those fair visions to annoy
Which seek utterance in thine eyes,
Memories of thy soul's pure rise—
Visions which consort with nought
Earth possesses, save in thought?
Jeamie, lad, with tearful face,
In thy lineaments I trace
There is grief in store for thee—
Thou art sure too like to me!
Life, my boy, may be a dream—
Thou dost think so, it doth seem—
Yet, withal, to men 'tis not:
Real—real—all their thought,
Haste and worry, toil and woe,
Fated lot of all below—
Most to such who will not go
With the busy onward flow,
But must stand, and gaze, and dream,
At the everlasting stream—
Dream and gaze with wondering mirth
At the turmoil of this earth.

Jamie, thou canst never guess
Thou, dear boy, dost suffer less,
When the rod corrective falls,
Than thy pa who hears thy calls:
Thou canst never know the smart,
Tearful troublings of the heart,
When I see thy upturned face

Raised to mine for pitying grace—
Hear thy cries, so like my own,
That I may thy faults condone.
I, my boy, have dreams like thine,
Dreams that ne'er with life combine,—
Struggling aspirations strong,
Which in vain for utterance long ;
Yet must ever onward go,
Nor one moment's resting know—
Vainly striving to repress
What I never may express ;
Mingling with the storm and strife,
Sternly sacrificing life—
Life within for death without,
Inward truth for outward doubt,—
All, my boy, that you and I
May not for a living die !—
Paradox both strange and quaint,
Cause and cure for one complaint !

Jeamie, Jeamie, thoughtful Jeamie !
Tearful, silent, wondering, dreamy :
Shouldst thou age of manhood reach,
And this life its lessons teach,—
Then, perchance, thou'lt understand
'Twas necessity's command
Urgéd him who shaped thy life
To prepare thee for its strife ;
Surely—surely, wilt forgive
Pains that made more fit to live—
Fitter with the wrong to fight,
Fitter to pursue the right,
Fitter to uphold thy soul
Till it reach its heavenly goal !

—◦✸◦—

MY LOVE, MY LOVE.

My love, my love, there's that in thee
   Doth make my life a dream,
An ever-running melody,
   An ever-singing stream.
A stream that runs to the sea,
   And in its depths is lost ;
In depths of harmony,
   Ne'er by a tempest toss'd.

'Tis day and night I run
   To this reposeful sea,
To thee, my darling one,
   Whose love is all for me.
Oh, clasp me in thy deeps,
   Sweep o'er me with thy waves,
Till in thy bosom sleeps
   The longing that now craves !

What though, on every side,
   The flowers droop o'er, to woo ?
To thee, my ocean bride,
   My course I swift pursue.
I sing, but 'tis of thee,
   I murmur but thy name—
'Tis thou the melody,
   And harmony the same.

A happy stream, I run,
   Forever to the sea ;
To thee, my darling one,
   In truest constancy.
Ope, ope, thy bosom, dear,
   With arms outspreading wide—
Without a thought, a fear,
   I'm lost in thee, my bride !

.:t.:

"WE ARE SUCH STUFF."

WHEN lovers meet to part again,
When sorrow comes with numbing pain,
When all our joys no longer please,—
What say the whisperings in the trees?
     "We'll love again to-morrow."

We'll love again: but what care I?
To-day we live, to-morn we die;
It is not much to say that we
Can live, and love, and cease to be,
     And love again to-morrow.

We live to love, nor care to say
That all our life should pass away
In hoping life itself should fly,
And with it, hopes and feelings die,
     To live again to-morrow:

Yet how is this, that we should care
To live, and love, and feel despair,
When all our life is but a dream,
And we, the dreamers, only seem
     To hope to wake to-morrow?

Belovéd visions, faint and grey,
More clear, more bright than open day!
Depart, ye certainties so fair,
I know you not, nor do I care
     If I shall wake to-morrow.

We may not be what else we might,
But this is clear, and pure, and bright:
Man is not what to man he seems,
And he that thinks so surely dreams.
     Perchance he'll wake to-morrow.

THE BALLAD OF LADY JANE.

"COME, busk thee, lass, the hour is nigh,
    The bridal hour, I ween,
When thou must wed Sir Ellerslie,
    The bravest knight e'er seen."

" How can I wed, though he may woo?"
    The daughter made reply ;
" Until my own true love return,
    A simple maid am I."

" Come, busk thee, lass, nor say me nay,
    Thy lover, where is he?
Thy father bids thee wed this night
    The brave Sir Ellerslie."

" Now, father, do not cruel be,
    Unto thy daughter dear,
For certainly I may not wed
    Until my love appear."

The baron stamped with iron foot
    Upon the oaken floor ;
He curs'd her love in Palestine,
    He curs'd his daughter more.

" Dost dare presume to thwart thy sire?
    Base child, I say to thee
This night thou dost become the bride
    Of brave Sir Ellerslie !"

Sweet Lady Jane turn'd sad away,
    And shed a silent tear ;
Her love was far across the sea,
    And succour none was near.

Run, run, dark river, to the sea,
    And in its bosom hide!
This night a woeful deed is done
    That well may shame thy tide!

'Tis Lady Jane stands on thy bank,
    Where often she had strayed,
A happy lover at her side,
    And she a happy maid.

The night is dark, the river deep,
    But nought of fear hath she;
" Farewell, my father dear," she cries,
    " Who could so cruel be!

" Farewell, farewell, my sweetheart dear,
    So far, so far away—
Would only thou from thy true love
    Had never sought to stray!"

The air is laden with the scent
    Of thyme and rosemarie,
And little birds within their nests
    Are sleeping peacefully.

But all alone, upon the bank,
    There stands a figure white—
Accurséd be that flowing tide,
    Accurséd be that night!

She leaps into the gurgling stream
    Without a sob or sigh—
Oh, tender must that maiden be,
    Who can but love or die!

Now, faithful collie, 'tis thy time,
    To show a noble breed—
Thy mistress dear in yonder stream
    Of thee hath surely need!

He springs—he seizes in his mouth
  Those locks of flowing gold,
And to the river bank doth bring
  His mistress wet and cold.

" Now hast thou done a cruel thing,
  For very love of me ;
Would thou hadst left me in yon stream
  To perish utterly !

" For what canst thou, my collie, know,
  Of anguish or distress ?
See'st thou the guests in yonder hall,
  And canst their purpose guess ?

" They wait their bride, thy mistress dear,
  And would her life enchain
To one who hath less love than thou,
  Who saved'st me in vain.

" Down, down, I prithee, faithful brute,
  And to thy couch repair !
Thy mistress hath such grief of heart
  As thou canst never share."

              *   *   *   *   *

Oh, is it ghost, or mist, or dream,
  Or vision of the night ?
Hath it fit substance for the form
  That hath that face so white ?

For hinds are gathered round the hearth,
  The day's dull labours done,
While song and jest move swiftly round,
  And merry is each one.

But hist ! " Didst hear that at the door ? "
  Each listener holds his breath,
But save the moaning of the wind,
  'Tis all as still as death.

"There 'tis again!—heard'st not that sound?"
  And to the cottage door
All eyes are turned with gaze of dread,
  And, gazing, dread the more.

The clock ticks loudly on the wall,
  The bird stirs in the cage,
The embers from the fireplace fall,
  Each moment seems an age.

Then see!—the handle of the door
  Is slowly turnéd round,
The door is gently openéd,
  Without the faintest sound.

What thing is this, that makes each hind
  His manliness forget?
A dog is thrust into the room,
  All shivering and wet!

A dog that whineth to escape,
  While one white trembling hand
Doth gently push him back again,
  With silent, sure command.

Then, dreadful sight!—while hearts stand still,
  A pale and ghastly face,
From which the water drippeth down,
  Doth meet their stonied gaze!

'Tis gone—the door is swiftly closed;
  'Twere sure a vision vain,
But for this trembling collie dog
  Of our sweet Lady Jane!

        *   *   *   *   *

"Ho! rouse, ye vassals, curs'd and slow,
  And seek the Lady Jane!
To him who our dear daughter finds
  Shall be this golden chain!

"Quick to our horse, Sir Ellerslie!
　Together forth we'll ride—
'Tis I to seek an only child,
　And thou a promised bride!"

They mount, away they ride in haste,
　But not a word speak they,
The father grieveth in his heart
　His cruel words that day.

"Would I but saw my daughter's face,
　And heard my daughter's voice!
Not all the lands of Ellerslie
　Should force her from her choice."

And what is this, all dripping white,
　That cometh on a bier?
The father uttereth never a word,
　Yet 'tis his daughter dear.

His daughter and his darling child,
　And who so fair as she!
The father kisses her wet, wet lips
　Yet not a tear sheds he.

Run, run, dark river, to the sea,
　And in its bosom hide!
What is a father's grief to thee,
　And what a promised bride?

For 'twas a maid who lived to love,
　And for her love did sigh;
Oh, tender was that maid, indeed,
　Who could but love or die!

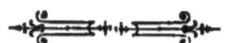

RONDELS.

I.—LOVE.

THE theme is old : I know it, dear—
As old as heaven itself, I'm told ;
And yet, I neither sigh nor fear
The theme is old !
I may be wrong, I may be bold,
To utter what is felt so near ;
Yet, do not thou my utterance scold,
Since thou in all I write appear ;
And never shall my song grow cold
In praise of love, although I hear
The theme is old !

II.—THE MORNING STAR.

THE morning star is fading in the blue,
As Phoebus mounts in flaming car,
From amorous climes, in haste to woo
The morning star.
And like a maiden pale at lattice bar
Awaiting tardy lover, who,
With sudden face upon her dreams doth jar,
And joy to trembling turn anew,
So, radiant orb, thy fervid love doth mar
The dreamings of thy mistress true,
The morning star.

III.—TO MY CHOIR.

SING out, my choir! What though in numbers weak?—
The heart to Heaven, it first doth Heaven require,
And in each trembling accent love doth speak—
Sing out, my choir!
Let tenderness and unity inspire,

As in the past, your ministry, and seek
From lowly, humble things, to climb to higher.
　　Whate'er our lot, life over—silent, meek,
We shall not, may not, question or inquire:
　　Yet is there pleasure in the thought, though weak,
That Heaven may grant to us this one desire,
　　To hear our great Conductor these words speak,
　　　　" Sing out, my choir!"

IV.—THE MOON IS HIGH.

THE moon is high, the night is still,
　　The glistening stars crowd in the sky:
Where now is death, or grief, or ill?
　　The moon is high!
Beneath the sun we throb and cry,
　　'Tis life we needs must, *will* or *nil*,
And earth doth move in all we try.
　　Oh, with thy placid spirit fill
My heart, fair moon, as thus I sigh,
　　With fondly-gazing, happy thrill,
　　The moon is high!

V.—TO MY LOVE ASLEEP.

SLEEP on, my dear, in rosy, dreamy ease,
　　Thou hast a faithful watcher near,
A watcher whom thy tranquil breathings please,
　　Sleep on, my dear!
Thy lover true, unseen, unknown, is here,
　　And feels thy breath, like fragrant breeze,
Upon his cheek ; and sips, 'twixt joy and fear,
　　The nectars of such lips as bees,
On honeyed quest intent, ne'er found the peer—
　　Who could resist such prize to seize?
　　Sleep on, my dear!

NIGHT AND DAY.

SLUMBROUS day and wakeful night
   Is the order of my life :
Whither shall I seek aright—
   In the silence or the strife ?

Waken thoughts and forms are dreams,
   Real dreamings real seem ;
From the darkness radiance streams
   Brighter than the sun's pale gleam.

Waken thoughts, I pray—away !
   Dreams, approach, that seem afar !
Hence, thou gaudy, tinselled day—
   Hither, hither, diamond star !

Glimmer in my darkness, star !
   'Tis a heaven that holds thee dear ;
Sun doth all our seeing mar,
   In the dark thou shinest clear !

A SCOTCHMAN'S SONNET.

HECH, sirs, the sonnet's but a fashious thing
   That gi'e's your poet wha has little sense
   O' ocht but jinglin' rhymes, sma' recompense
For a' the labours that his jinglin's bring !
Ye crack aboot your poets wha can sing
   O' love an' joy, in ilka mood an' tense,
   Or haver o' sic thochts an' things immense
As a' but poets' comprehensions ding :
But gi'e's the lad can roon' a denty sonnet,
   An' no forget to pit intil't a thocht !
What tho' he think it richt to cock his bonnet ?
   We'll no begrudge the sma' bit credit socht ;
Gin he's nae poet, tak' my word upon it,
   He has the stuff frae whilk a poet's wrocht !

E R O S.

THOUGH oft the Poet thought pursue
To depths refined, remote from view,
One theme alone commands my will,
And ever onward urges still !
In vain a wayward, grovelling sense
In baser themes seeks recompense
For inward aspirations spurned,
And welling streamlets backward turned :
The channel chokes, the waters rise,
Then comes a swift, a sweet surprise :
While earth engages every thought,
Kind heaven approaches all unsought—
An angel stirs the waters deep,
Away all barriers they sweep !
I hear the fluttering wings above,
Look up, and scorn all themes but love !

The gentle dew descends from heaven—
Who knoweth all the dew hath given ?
That dew distills on parchéd earth,
And beauteous flowers smile at their birth ;
Ethereal, tender winds of thought
Breathe round the Poet's head, unsought ;
He stretches nervous hands to grasp
At hidden mysteries, or clasp
The forms evanishing in mist,
Like glimmering stars by morning kissed—
'Tis all in vain, they further fly,
And silence clasps him with a sigh.
Oh, linger near me, Heavenly power !
Protect, forgive me in that hour
When I, forgetful, wandering stray
From consciousness of thee away !
I know indeed, I know, I know,

'Tis thought alone flits to and fro,
While 'neath this consciousness of earth
There goeth on eternal birth—
The seeming of ourselves we see,
But never can the real *we;*
Around, above, beneath, we gaze,
Behold a universe ablaze,
Each soul itself a central sun,
Round which the lesser satellites run ;
Each seeing all he can aright,
Yet all his seeing as his sight :
He and the orbs that round him run
But twinkling to a hidden sun—
The centre of the heavens he feels,
Yet circling round another wheels!

The mystery fills my heart with peace,
As cords that bind too fast, release,
And heaven's infinitudes of space
Are to our dullness commonplace.
I pray to one who hears my voice—
He gives the utterance of my choice ;
From depths within comes longing cry—
A simple emanation I !
'Tis but a feebleness of sight
That questioneth the noon-day light,
And in the radiance of that day
Begotten of the primal ray,
This simple order doth prevail—
The seer is invisible :
What is created, forward goes,
The creature to creator grows—
Forever onward flows the stream
Of life, and thought, and shifting dream :
The vast infinitudes are ours,
Faint adumbrations of our powers—
All, all we see but satellites,

While we ourselves, the central lights,
From still, invisible brightness spring—
Mysterious, wondrous ordering!

Forward, my soul! I see my world!
Like heaven's own shaft, from darkness hurled,
There flashes on my inward sight,
The truth that all I see is right :
That all I see is but my own,
The faint harmonics of a tone.
Oh, pure I would the music be
That rests its harmonies on me!
Tune me, O Love, unseen, unknown—
Dost thou not breathe, is this my moan?
I hear, I tremble, I prepare!
Impassionate, impassive air,
I yield me to thy melting will—
Speak me, thy word, and love fulfill
In swelling chords of heavenly song,
And grant me power to make men long!

——◦❈❈◦——

AND WE?

THERE'S not a flower,
    Come, dear, away,
We have no power
    To stay decay.
Die, die they must,
    Die all we see :
They are but dust,
    And we?—and we?

There's not a flower,
    Come, come away,
We have no power

The tale how well
In all we see:
But who can tell
So well as we?

There's not a flower—
Away, away—
We have no power
To stay decay.
'Tis thus with all,
With all we see,
And as they fall,
So, soon shall we.

——◦✠◦——

WHAT THE RIVER SAYS.

RIVER, river, softly flowing,
Whither, whither, are we going,
Thou and I?
" To the sea, the sea, to the sea away—
We may not dally or delay,
Thou and I."

River, river, softly flowing,
Wherefore to the sea are going
Thou and I?
" From the sea, the sea, from the sea we came,
And to it return, though not the same,
Thou and I."

River, river, softly flowing,
Shall we then lose all our knowing,
Thou and I?
" Never, never, doubting one,
For through eternity shall run
Thou and I."

L I F E ?

WHETHER we live, or whether we die,
There *is* a heaven for those who sigh,
  A haven sure of quiet rest
  For hearts with troublous doubts oppress'd,
A joy for those who sob and cry.

Whether we live, or whether we die—
It seemeth one to those who sigh :
  This life of ours, so short a breath,
  Were sure more fitly calléd death :
We do but live in hope to die.

Whether we live, or whether we die—
Two thoughts diverging still more nigh :
  Proceeding east, we reach the west,
  And in unquiet find our rest :
We long for life, for death we sigh.

Whether we live, or whether we die,
Earth hath no life for those who sigh ;
  Let death be ours, 'tis all we crave,
  Nor seek we aught from life to save :
O death, restore our life, we cry.

W E E D S.

THOU Heaven that send'st thy gentle rain,
On humble weed as well as grain,
Hast surely some becoming use
For what men only find abuse.
Perchance, the flowers and fruits which grace
And decorate sweet Nature's face,

Which please and gratify each sense,
Have, in their being recompense
For all the pleasures they bestow
On longing mortals here below ;
But wherefore power of being given,
Soft balmy airs and dews from heaven,
To such as men can only spurn,
If Heaven doth look for no return ?
Assure thyself, O mortal vain,
There's not a weed that dots the plain
Of human life, or flecks the corn,
A fitting object of thy scorn.
Oh, human hearts, though faint and low,
Have other purpose than we know ;
Heaven is the start, the strength, the end—
The goal towards which all beings tend,
And though none may life's purpose tell,
Heaven's purpose worketh there as well.

DEATH?

THIS careless thing, that lies so still,
    So calmly nothing—'tis a jest :
Who says *he* lies before us, will
    Arouse but tearful mirth at best.

With pick and spade let earth be rent,
    Quick to your work, put earth to earth ;
'Tis done, 'tis well : this body lent,
    Is now returned for second birth.

For birth—for birth ? We pause in thought :
    What birth hath he who late knew ours ?
This shuffling state, hath't meaning ought ?
    Is this our life ? are these our powers ?

Smoothe down the turf, make earth look fair,
  Plant flowers and trees upon his grave ;
Return, return ! life needs us there,
  There's nought on earth from death can save.

Lift high the voice in careless song,
  Renounce thy grief, let weeping go ;
As long as life holds on, so long
  We never can true living know.

————◦❧◦————

A HAND.

I.

WHEREVER I look, I see,
  But what see I ?
A Hand that beckons to me
From out of the mist—*To be ;*
And all that I hear is a cry,
Is—" Live, live live, that thou may'st die ! "

II.

Wherever I love, 'tis pain,
  But what care I ?
To suffer in love is gain,
If only this Hand remain,
And all that I hear in the cry,
Is—" Love, love, love, until thou die ! "

III.

Wherever I look, I see,
  And what see I ?
But this Hand that beckons to me.
I wave back my hand to thee !—
Lead onward, lead upward, I cry,
I follow thee, Love, till I die !

'TIS ALL OR NONE.

'Tis all or none, my pretty dear,
  So please you as it may!
For in sweet love, it doth appear,
  The absolute holds sway:
'Tis yes or no, a smile or frown,
The hopes that soar or fluttering drown!

I gave my love a beauteous rose
  When blushed the early morn,
A lily gave at evening's close,
  Yet both she laughed to scorn;
Heigho! 'twas labouring love in vain,
As cold as ice she did remain.

" 'Tis well!" I whispered to my heart,
  " That she should treat me so:
The hand that gives the quivering smart
  The cure alone should know;
And wavering love is not for me,
Now hot, now cold, now bound, now free."

My love returned, my love in tears,
  I kissed her tears away;
Her heart was mine beneath her fears,
  And love had gained the day!
And love once given can ne'er return,
Its fires once lit, forever burn!

Z Ō N A N Ē ;

OR,

THE FIDDLE WIZARD OF CREMONA.

A LEGEND. *ๆนๅ.*

In old Cremona, fiddle-famed,
Once lived my hero, Strombo named.
Down in a narrow, dingy street,
Where toppling houses seem to meet,
With many a quaint old balustrade,
And corniced window strangely made,
With goblin griffins grim and grey,
That stretch across the narrow way,
As if the builders, in their thought,
For far contingencies had wrought,
When times should trouble, wars be rife,
And trembling fugitives for life
Might leap from griffin-head or scroll
Right o'er the gap, to safety's goal ;
Or planned, perchance, with purpose sweet,
How Romeos might their Juliets meet,
And, 'cross the broken arch above,
Leap into welcoming arms of love ;
Where scarce a streak of Italian sky
Can e'en be seen by passers-by,
And everything around is quaint,
Filling the mind with visions faint
Of times and beings scarce of earth
That could these structures strange give birth ;
Where even the dreamy dwellers seen
Seem less to be, than to have been,
And shuffle along their daily round
With scarce a motion or a sound—
Ghosts of a race and of an age

Whose glories live on history's page,
Poor silent shadows of the past,
By its refulgent brightness cast :—
Here, wrought in secret and at ease
My fiddle wizard Cremonese !

His was the house with oaken door,
Encarved fantastically o'er :
Slow on its rusty hinge it swings,
As if to some dead past it clings,
And, under some religious vow,
Would bar us from admission now.
Quick through this lobby, dark and low,
Up this slim staircase, let us go :
Behold the room, the very spot,
Where once our master thought and wrought !
Canst see it with the inward eye,
And round, in strange confusion, lie
The jostled fragments which shall yet
By magic subtlety beget
Such ravishing, such heavenly strains
As lead a weeping world in chains ?
Here, at his bench, the master stood,
And wrought his miracles in wood—
With art which all the world defied
O'ercame where other men but tried ;
Disturbed the common place of men
By ways and modes beyond their ken,
Till scarce a being in the town
Would pass the house when sun was down ;
While teeth would chatter, legs would quake,
If force compelled that way to take,
And many a fearful glance they'd throw,
And *Ave Maria*, faint and low,
With holy crossings, murmur fast,
As Strombo's house they hurried past !
Then, what weird sounds would stir the night

From slumbers deep to wakeful fright—
What lights would flicker to and fro
With strange unearthly gleam and glow—!
Not heaven or earth, the people said,
Gave Strombo's skill of hand and head !

Renown'd o'er all the world was he
For feats of fiddle-surgery,
And lands afar rejoiced to tell
How he could make ill fiddles well—
Renew the youth of veterans aged,
And free tone-secrets centuries caged.
Here fiddles came both great and small,
Fiddles for street, for court, and ball ;
Fiddles one might have made to speak,
Fiddles whose mission was to squeak ;
Fiddles with lengthy pedigree,
Fiddles of very low degree ;
Fiddles for kings, by masters made,
Fiddles by wandering minstrels played :
Here came their lords, from east and west,
From north and south, with same request :

"O Fiddle-mender, take good care,
And my Cremona well repair !
There's not a fiddle in the land
(As you and I well understand)
Is worth a ducat but my own—
With such a figure, varnish, tone,
Such fine proportions, splendid wood—
Be careful, Fiddle-mender good,
And exercise your finest art
On what has not its counterpart."

Thus spoke they all, each fiddler glad
He only perfect fiddle had ;
While all were courteously received,
And all—apparently—believed.

No matter though the "instrument"
For fiddling ends had ne'er been meant,
But made with simple view to sell,
And might have been a tub as well,
A coffin, chair, or bunch of sticks—
Old Strombo never was in fix !
He'd praise each fiddle to the skies,
Declare each owner had a prize,
Which he would guard with jealous care,
And in a fitting style repair ;
Then, should they grumble at the price,
Our master had them in a trice—
Would swift recount the virtues o'er
Which owners had extolled before,
And, gathering up the ducats bright,
Would blandly put them out of sight :
" Such works of art need artful aid,
And art, dear Signor, must be paid ! "

But how he'd smile when all alone,
And, muttering in exulting tone,
Step to the secret closet there,
Take thence a case with tender care,
And from the case, where shrined it lay,
Bring forth the fiddle *Zonanē!*
Then would he soft apostrophise
This one inestimable prize :

" O *Zonanē*, thy magic spell
Doth work exceedingly and well !
From every land beneath the sun
Behold the crowd of fiddlers run !
All seeking aid which none can give
Should thou and I but cease to live.
Ha, treasure of mine eyes and ears,
What mystery in thy form appears !
When, from the precious fragments riven
From many an ancient fiddle given

By mourning owners to my care,
To make some requisite repair,
I built thee by such subtle skill
As baffles all my thinking still—
I little knew the magic power
With which thou shouldst thy maker dower!
By secret means, in secret taught,
From fiddle fragments thou wert wrought;
Yet, more than mortal man could plan,
Yea, more than wildest dreams of man,
Art thou, my matchless *Zonanē*,
When o'er thy strings my bow doth stray!
King of all fiddle-menders I,
And dread *Ponēron's* power defy!
Come when he will, with purpose stern,
He'll find he has some things to learn—
With thee, *Ponēron's* power is nought,
There's more in thee than ere he thought!"

One night—'tis many years ago—
Old Strombo stood communing so;
While torrents poured and lightnings flashed,
And noisy thunders rolled and crashed,
He stood, unheeding, where we stand,
With that strange fiddle in his hand.

"Quick to thy task, brave *Zonanē*,
There's work before us ere the day!
See'st not the mob that's gathered round?
A hundred fiddlers, I'll be bound,
Are at this moment fretting fain
To hear again the welcome strain
Of their own fiddles, sound and well,
Which now of shattered systems tell.
Ha, ha! behold a motley lot—
What dire disorder have they not?
Here, battered ribs and broken head,

There, spinal weakness, heart of lead,
Intestines gone, and liver slow,
Some minus head, or tail below ;
That one, consumptive, sunken chest,
With head reclining on his breast ;
Here one, poor soul ! has lost his head,
And got another one's instead ;
Some gaping with a hundred rents,
Or battered out of shape with dents—
All calling for our aid and will,
Come, *Zonanē*, display thy skill !"

Then, to that chin, which seemed to say,
"Come, tuck thee in, sweet fiddle, pray !"
The fiddle-wonder see him raise,
And down upon it fondly gaze,
While in his fingers, long and thin,
The bow he clutches to begin :
One moment see him gaze around
Before the mystery profound
Shall be enacted o'er again—
Bewilderment of fiddle-men !
One moment, while the mass confused
Of fiddles battered and abused
He scans with comprehensive eye,
His fiddle set, and bow on high—
Then, with a touch as soft, as light,
As snowflakes falling in the night,
Across the strings the bow see slip,
From tip to heel, from heel to tip,
From *largo*, slow, to *presto*, fast—
Each bowing quicker than the last—
The longer playing, hurrying more,
Until his arm seemed like a score !

What ravishment of heavenly sound
Swells on the pulsing air around !

The very fiddles strewn about
First throb and stir—then, in and out,
Rush whirling round weird *Zonanē*
While Strombo still goes on to play!
Fantastic order reigns around—
A geometric kind of sound,
Begotten of the magic spell
The fiddle wizard works so well.
Then, slackening speed and dropping bow,
Behold a greater wonder now:
Each fiddle that had joined the throng,
Borne by the magic strains along—
No matter what its ills had been,
Is now in perfect order seen;
The spinal weakness all is gone,
Consumptive fiddles there are none,
And fiddles erst without a head,
Or with some other one's instead,
Have somehow now their own regained;
While fiddles battered, splintered, stained,
Shine with a mellow amber glow
Which all true fiddlers love and know,
Each fiddle perfect, sound, and whole,
By *Zonanē's* occult control!

But ah, my Strombo, master thou
Of arts not named by mortals now—
There's one behind thee thou dost know—
Prepare, O Strombo—thou must go!
The wizard turns, and face to face,
Beholds the foe of human race—
His most Satanic Majesty,
With folded arms and leering eye,
Cap jauntily on one side set,
From which waved feather black as jet,
One foot advanced, and chest thrown out—
A figure quaint enough, no doubt!

He spoke in accents low and calm,
While Strombo heard without a qualm.

"That's well, my Strombo, that is well!
Your _Zonanē_ hath still its spell,
And everything, so far's I know,
And as reported down below,
Has been exactly as agreed,
And I'm from further waiting freed.
So now, my dear old fellow, come,
Your time is up, and there is some
Short distance for us both to go
Before we reach my place below ;
Besides, to let you understand,
I've other engagements still on hand ! "

" Begone, foul fiend, and quit my sight !
Ha, thou'rt mistaken far this night
If thou imaginest to touch,
With single crooked claw as much,
My _Zonanē_, or even myself,
Thou lying, plundering, knavish elf !
Ha, ha, my fiend, be not so quick !
Thou hast forgotten there's a trick
Which _Zonanē_ can work as well
As any fiddle-mending spell !
And while it waves 'twixt thee and me,
A fig for all the powers that be ! "

" What ho, old Strombo ! why so wroth,
Or to accompany me so loth ?
Did I not show the secret way
To make confounded _Zonanē_ ?
Hast thou not had thy soul's desire,
And shall I want what I require ?
Quick ! fly ! thou fiddle-mender old !
I'll take thee where thou'lt ne'er feel cold,
And, if you'll only quick away,

I'll let you take your *Zonanē !* ''

    " Begone ! " old Strombo cried, " begone ! "

    " Come on ! " the fiend replied, " come on ! "

    Then came a struggle, brief but dire !
The fiend sprang forward in his ire,
And thought old Strombo's throat to seize
With all simplicity and ease,
But back he started, stormed, and raved,
While in his face old Strombo waved
The magic fiddle *Zonanē,*
And dared him as he stood at bay !

    " I'll settle that, my nice old man,
Although you scarcely think I can !
That fellow there behind your back
Will set you on another track ! "

    Alas, alas ! Old Strombo turned !—
There was a flash—a puff—and burned
And charred, in smoking fragments, lay
The wonder-fiddle *Zonanē!*
One instant Strombo stood amazed,
Clasped both his hands and downward gazed,
A sigh, a groan, a shake of head,
And poor old Strombo's soul had fled !

     *   *   *   *   *   *   *

    Then runs the legend. Far and near,
A thousand fiddles, 'twould appear,
Which Strombo had some time put right,
Went into splinters that same night ;
A thousand fiddlers ran with speed
To good old Strombo in their need ;
And here, within this very room,
Where evening shadows gathering gloom,
Stretched on a pile of fiddles old,
They found our master stiff and cold !

THE WANDERER.

WHERE'ER I wander o'er the earth,
The land of Scotland and my birth
   I never can forget :
Within my heart, like dew in rose,
Or pearl the greedy shells enclose,
   Or star in heaven, 'tis set !

Is't o'er Arabia's desert waste
That now with trembling steps I haste
   Before the dread Simoom ?
Or in the silent frigid zone
I wander 'midst the ice alone,
   In strange ethereal gloom ?

'Tis then, thou land I love so well,
Thine influence moves me as a spell,
   Thy beauties on me rise !
To heath-clad hills and pebbly burns,
To woods and glens, my spirit turns,
   And lives on memories !

And when, on nobler Indian strand,
With nature's love on every hand,
   I wander on, at ease,—
My thoughts to wander still refuse,
Upon one theme I ever muse—
   'Tis thou alone canst please !

And though an exile I must stray
From thee, my native land, away,
   Howe'er so dear I love ;
Yet, land of home, I'm ever thine—
For thee I pray, for thee I pine,
   Scotland, all lands above !

THE LASS THAT SANDY LO'ES.

THE siller mune is in the sky,
　The corn is stackit cheerie, O,
An' I'll across the stubby field,
　To see my bonnie dearie, O!
　　Hech, lads, but she's the lass to lo'e,
　　An' weel I ken her hairt is true,
　　Wi' her I carena tho' the noo
　　　The warl' gaed tapselteerie, O!

There's Jock an' Tam the pleuch can haud,
　The grubber an' the harrows, O,
An', gin mysel', the country roon',
　Ye'll hardly fin' their marrows, O.
　　I ken my wark an' dae it weel,
　　I like to airn my milk an' meal,
　　To maister an' to man I'm leal,
　　　In bothie an' in furrows, O!

But tak' my bonnie Jean awa',
　An' upside down ye'll turn me, O;
Just tie me wi' a wisp o' straw,
　An' coup me in the burnie, O!
　　Guid life, my lads, it's no in man
　　To dae ocht mair than ocht he can—
　　The lassies fill the butter-pan,
　　　An' we are but the chirnie, O!

I'll wrasle wi' ye, ony twa,
　This neive can stoon a stirkie, O;
The de'il himsel', wi' horns an' tail,
　Wad hardly fricht this birkie, O!
　　But Jeannie has sic winnin' way,
　　Gin she but will, wha can say nay?
　　It's heicht o' freedom to obey,
　　　Without a doot or quirkie, O!

Hech, but the mune shines bricht the nicht,
  My heart is liltin' rarely, O!
I'll no gae hame till mornin' licht,
  Gin Jeannie treats me fairly, O!
    An' she's the lass I dearly lo'e,
    For her I'd trudge the hail warl' through,
    An ne'er sall grudge a swatty broo,
      Or toil baith late an early, O!

OH, TELL ME NOT.

Oh, tell me not, in measured strain,
We may not, cannot, love again,
That hearts are cold, if lips are still,
And only what we know, we will!

Not in mere freedom of my verse,
Believe me, dear, would I rehearse
The truth that love can never die,
The truth, my dear, nor know the why.

I feel, I love: I am, thou art,
And each to each the counterpart;
Suffice it, love, we love indeed,
Faint words can ne'er express love's need.

Still, still those lips! a kiss will seal
A meaning more than words reveal;
Thine, thine I am, and mine thou art,
And weak the love which words impart!

Once more.

R A I N.

RAIN, rain, rain,
How it floods the thirsty plain !
And the flowers look up,
To fill each tiny cup,
And drink them to the bottom that they may be filled
again !

Here, the cows among the grass
Never see you as you pass,
But crop, crop, crop,
And let the rain-beads drop
From ears, and tail, and nose,
Without a single heed :
Yet not a drop down-flows
But hath of thanks its meed.

And the brook runs merrily down the hill,
O'er-gushing with boisterous pleasure,
There's nothing can stop its torrent until
It empties itself without measure
Into the stately-flowing stream
That o'er the plain doth run ;
For it its wavelets gleam
In rising and setting of sun.
To reach the stream it dashes
Adown the hill,
And o'er the boulders splashes
With resolute will.
Until it glides along the verdant plain,
Where drooping willows twine,
And blackbirds pipe their mellow strain,
With lowing of drowsy kine.

And the hills roll down their white and gleamy mist
Upon the plain,

And proudly lift their brows by sunshine kissed,
    And bathed in rain.
While the scented fringe of Nature's robe, the flowers,
    Breathe incense sweet
To gracious Heaven for these refreshing showers
    And grateful heat.
And noisy sparrows chirp beneath the eaves
    And watch the rain
Run dripping down the drooping glistening leaves,
    And cheer the grain.

    And while the welcome rain
    Streams o'er the thirsty plain,
The children scamper in and out ;
    And men gaze to the heaven,
    Whence all this joy is given,
And raise on high harmonious shout—-

    " The rain, rain, rain,
    Hath come again !
    There's pleasure in the earth,
    And plenty for our dearth ;
    There's fruitfulness and ease,
    And everything to please
      In the coming of the rain !
    We'll lift our grateful voice
      In praise again—
    Rejoice, rejoice, rejoice,
      For this glad rain ! "

SCOTLAND.

SCOTLAND! there's trembling at my heart
   Thy name alone can bring,
Be mine, be mine, the honoured part
   Of thee, my land, to sing!
To sing of all thou art and hast
   For us who own thy name,
Our fathers loved thee in the past—
   Their children's love's the same!
For thee they bled and freely died,
And we would share their noble pride!

Around our lives there twines a grace
   By thy kind fingers thrown,
There is reflected in our face
   A spirit not our own.
Thy secret influence nerves each limb
   That throbs with conscious worth,—
We know, we feel, though faint and dim,
   Through thee, our land of birth,
There breathes in us the eternal soul
Which swayeth all, with sweet control.

Before thy hills that kiss the sky,
   As in thy forests deep,
We feel the silent ministry
   Thou constantly dost keep;
What treasure can our hearts desire
   If thou be only ours?
What spirit can our hearts inspire
   That equals thine own powers?
We scorn all themes but love and thee,
Scotland, the beautiful and free!

Hand grasped in hand, ye brothers, then,
   Our voices mingling raise,

The heavens shall echo back again
　　Our noble country's praise !
For us the meads and fragrant flowers,
　　The streams, the mountains strong—
Where'er we gaze, 'tis ours, 'tis ours,
　　The land of love and song !
Oh, noble should the spirits be
Which own, dear Scotland, birth to thee !

------o-❧-o------

A WITHERED ROSE.

A ROSE, a rose, a withered rose,
　　Saved from the faded years,
On one soft summer evening's close
　　Bestowed with vows and tears.

" What shall I give thee, love," he said,
　　" This night I part from thee ? "
I smiled, with heart that drooped and bled,
　　And said, " That rose give me."

I knew how soon would be forgot
　　The promises he made,
I saw this day, yet murmured not,
　　Nor did I aught upbraid.

He gave the rose, and turned away :
　　'Tis many a year ago,
The locks he praised are tinged with grey,
　　And all alone I go.

OUR HARRY.

ÆTAT. 3.

SLEEPY, sleepy, curly head,
Down upon your lazy bed—
Arms outstretched in warm repose,
Cheeks as red as summer rose !—
Don't you see the sun is high,
And your ma is standing by,
Waiting till her darling boy
Ope his eyes with start of joy?
    Harry, sleepy Harry !

There you are ! just see the sun—
Long ago his work's begun !
Hear the birds, too, 'neath the eaves,
And the rustling of the leaves !
See yon river swiftly flow,
Feel the winds that come and go—
All the world is broad awake,
Up you get, and breakfast take,
    Harry, lazy Harry !

Now you're up ! downstairs we'll go—
Put your arms about me, so ;
What a time you've been in bed,
Sleepy, sleepy, sleepy head !
Pa, just see your boy at last,
Wakened from his slumbers fast ;
What's the forfeit he should pay?
Kisses round is what I say,
    Harry, cosy Harry !

Breakfast's over, then to play,
Scamper in and out all day ;
Shouting, singing, whistling clear—
That's our Harry that you hear !

Who gave you that pretty rose?
'Twas "A lady 'at me knows!"
Who gave all those sweets I see?
'Twas "A man 'at speaks to me!"
  Harry, funny Harry!

Never utter single word,
Or if Harry's near, 'tis heard;
Never secret thing impart—
Harry has it all by heart!
Eyes and ears are open wide,
If you're wrong, then woe betide!
Err but from the truth one bit,
Harry tells you, "'at's not it!"
  Harry, watchful Harry!

Then, 'tis all that pa or ma
Does or utters, is his law:
Pa, unmindful, may forget
Where he put his cigarette,
Harry thinks he'll have a puff—
"Put that down!" comes order rough;
Down it goes, with answer pat,
"Ma, I seen mine pa do 'at!"
  Harry, wilful Harry!

If you're reading, Harry's there,
Clambering up upon your chair;
There's his head upon your book,
Gazing up with artful look!
If you're writing—all the same—
Harry's at his little game:
"Stop 'at writing, look at me,"
Hear him murmur at your knee,
  Harry, petted Harry!

Now he's scrambling up pa's breast,
Till his head the roof has pressed;

Now he's reading in a " book,"
With most philosophic look ;
Or he's singing "doh-me-fah,"
With approving "'at's it, pa !"
Ready to be taught or shown
What he thinks ought to be known,
    Harry, willing Harry !

And such messages he'll go,
(He is such a man, you know !)
Round the corner, down the street,
There our Harry you may meet ;
Now to fetch his pa some stamps,
Or his ma the bread, he tramps ;
Whistling all the way he goes,
Telling everyone he knows,
    Harry, clever Harry !

That's " him " with his head all bare,
Curly, yellow, golden hair ;
That's him with the eyes as bright
As the stars on frosty night ;
That's him with the laughing face,
Full of confidence and grace :
Who is't doesn't Harry know ?
Known and loved where'er he go,
    Harry, darling Harry !

That's " him " looking at the stars
Through the slits in lattice bars ;
That's him climbing on the chair,
Wondering at the moon up there !
Wondering if she's in her " ba,"
When the clouds about her draw ;
That's him in his cot at last,
Locked in smiling slumbers fast,
    Harry, bonnie Harry !

Dream thou on, my darling one !
Life with thee is but begun ;
Treasure up in childhood's years
Happiness for coming tears ;
Nothing on this earth, my boy,
Has such sweet, such lasting joy,
As the thoughts to childhood given—
Memories of thy homeland, Heaven !
    Harry, dear, dear, Harry !

I'LL SEE YE IN THE GLOAMIN'.

O LASSIE wi' the bonnie feet,
An' kilted skirt sae trim an' neat,
Gin ye a lad wad care to meet,
    I'll see ye in the gloamin'.

O laddie wi' the wistfu' e'e,
I thank ye for your thochts o' me,
But I ha'e ne'er a thocht to see
    A gowk like ye at gloamin' !

O lassie wi' the snawy broo,
The cheeks sae reid an' een sae blue,
I canna live for thochts o' you,
    At mornin', noon, an' gloamin'.

O laddie, ye're nae lad ava !
Gin ye had thochts o' love at a'
Ye wadna staun' sae far awa',
    An' crack 'aboot the gloamin' !

O lassie, weel ye kent me true,
Sae, cuddle in my bosie noo—
My faith, I'll pree your saucy mou',
    At mornin', noon, an' gloamin' !

THE TRYSTIN' TREE.

'TWAS in the munelicht Willie came,
    An' took me in his arms,
My face was glowin' hot wi' shame,
    My hairt was a' alarms.

" Gae, Willie, gae, nor seek to bide,
    Since your fause love has tined,
An' whaur ye gae, may guid betide,
    Though ye ha'e been unkind."

" Are they your thochts, my bonnie dear,
    That ye should speak sae wae?
An' ha'e ye ocht in me to fear,
    That I awa' maun gae?"

I looked intill my Willie's een,
    Oh, surely they were true,
An' a' the thochts I had yestreen
    Micht weel ha'e vanished noo!

But wha can mak' their love their ain,
    Or guide it to their will?
Although love reived my heart wi' pain,
    'Twas dour an' thrawn still.

" I kenna, Willie, hoo to say't,
    I kenna what I feel,
But you an' I can never mate,
    Though I ha'e lo'ed ye weel."

Doon on his face shone bricht the mune,
    His bannet aff his broo,
He loot my haun' fa' saftly doon,
    Wat wi' a tearfu' dew.

He turned awa', nor cuist his een
  To her wha lo'ed him dear:
"Love in thy hairt, lass, ne'er has been,
  Gin ye ha'e siccan fear."

He's gaen an' left me a' my lane,
  An' oh, my hairt was sair!
"Come back, kind Willie, come again,
  An' I'll ne'er doot thee mair!"

On through the yett an' doon the lane,
  He heedless took his way,
My feet to follow him were fain,
  An' yet ahint maun stay.

An' here, the nicht, aneath the tree
  Whaur aften we ha'e met,
I mourn owre a' that used to be,
  For love can ne'er forget.

"Nor shall it need, my ain kind dear—
  'Tis Willie cries to thee!
For noo ye ha'e the vision clear
  Tried love alane can gi'e!

"I'll clasp ye in my fond embrace,
  I'll kiss awa' your tears,
An' trustfu' love shall tak' the place
  O' a' your doots an' fears."

LOVE'S WARFARE.

THE air was still, the sun was high,
And at our own sweet will
We wandered on, my love and I,
Beside the purling rill.

" Come, seat thee, love, beside me here,
Among these cowslips pale,
And while I lend attentive ear,
Discourse me some sweet tale !"

" And what, my love," I swift replied,
" Shall be the favoured theme ?"
" Aught in this universe so wide,
Save one—thy constant dream."

" Save love, sweetheart ?   So be it, then,
Thou'lt choose the theme for me."
" Oh—sing of deeds of kingly men—
Some tale of chivalry."

" Thy will is mine, thy will is right,
Thy will must be obeyed ;
I'll tell thee of a noble knight—"
" Who loved a pretty maid !"

" Well, yes, he did, I recollect,
So, let that stupid go ;
The next I'll try to keep correct,
Since you desire it so.

" This was a knight who wore a glove,
When to the wars he went—"
" And, doubtless, 'twas his lady-love
Him to the wars had sent !"

" And so it was, I do declare—
    That theme again so stale ! .
Keep off, keep off, ye maidens fair,
    And let me tell my tale !"

" 'Tis very well to cry so loud,
    But don't you err again ;
Two chances only are allowed,
    Keep to your subject—men !"

" Well, this time 'twas a goodly knight
    Who fought upon a field,
And, with uplifted sword of might,
    Cried to his foeman, ' Yield !'

" The foeman yields, is prisoner ta'en,
    The knight hath won the day——"
" But why did all these knightly men
    Delight in battle fray ?"

" Why, why ?   Thou darling, stupid one,
    Who will not own 'tis true—
Because, although for-honour done,
    'Twas all—for love of you !"

" What mean you sir, that riddle so,
    And puzzle me for nought ?"
" Why, simply, that 'twas I, you know,
    Who thought what you had thought !"

" Well, that is simple, to be sure ;
    The sphinx were plain to read
Could I make sense of nonsense pure,
    Such as your thoughts, indeed !"

" Ah, Jasmine dear, a summer day
    May tell a dreadful tale,
When maids, equipped in love's array,
    Poor mortal men assail !"

" Hush, Phil, keep to romance,
    And come not nearer, pray,
For nearness never does enhance,
    And distance does, they say."

" I'm going, then—good-bye, good-bye !"
    " Stop, Phil, I'll go with you—
I'm sure you know as well as I,
    I love you, yes—I do !"

" What, 'pon your word, my dear, is't so?
    Then, seal it with a kiss ;
I think 'tis rather good, you know,
    To make it up like this !"

" Oh, Phil, you sly one !   Now I see
    'Twas all intended quite
To speak of cruelly leaving me,
    And put me in a fright."

" Well, darling mine, you won't deny
    It had the effect desired ;
But now I think both you and I
    Of war in love are tired.

" I know 'tis love you wish to hear,
    Yet love I must not speak :
Just say we'll marry in a year—"
    " A year, dear Phil ?   A week !"

WHEN THE MORNING SUN.

WHEN the morning sun is breaking
   Through the curtains of the night,
When the merry birds, up-waking,
   Mount to welcome in the light ;
When the lark is earthward sending,
   From his post at morning's gates,
All the love his bosom rending,
   While upon his bride he waits—
Then with love as pure, as free,
Throbs my heart at thought of thee.

When the sun at eve reposes
   On his crimson throne, a king,
And, like worshippers, the roses,
   At his feet their censers swing ;
When the moon, as one forsaken,
   Floating sadly through the night,
By the morn, her love, o'ertaken,
   Faints away in sweet delight—
Then my heart, at thought of thee,
Faints with love-born ecstasy.

Sweetheart, dearest, treasure-laden,
   Hast thou e'er a thought for me ?
Does thy bosom, gentle maiden,
   Ever throb, as mine for thee ?
Brightness of the sunrise glory,
   Sweetness of the breath of flowers—
Faery queen of olden story,
   Gently wield thy witching powers !
Let me not despairing pine,
Kiss me now, and say thou'rt mine !

Round thy head, in wavelets, smoothly
   Tresses fair and silky flow,

'Neath bent eye-brows beam full soothly
   Eyes not meant to slay, I trow;
Cheeks that flush with love's own brightness,
   As the heart-tides ebb and flow,
Teeth of pearly glistening whiteness,
   Lips that tempt the longer so!—
Queen of love! from thy degree,
Stoop to him who loves but thee!

SPRING SONG.

SING, sing, my darling, sing!
It is the merry Spring,
   And all is tender gladness;
The lark is in the sky,
On sea of melody,
A thousand voices round us cry,
   "Away with winter's sadness!"

Beneath the blossoming trees
We'll wander on at ease,
   And taste of Nature's pleasure,
We'll wander, happy pair,
And breathe the fragrant air:
Spring in our hearts, Spring everywhere,
   And joy withouten measure.

Sing, sing, my darling, sing!
It is the merry Spring,
   The Spring for pleasure given;
Up with the lark on high
On wings of love we fly,
Of love and song, love, thou and I,
   Until we reach yon heaven!

THAT NIGHT.

Two flowers I gave my love that night
  Of happy dance and song,
A lily, for her tresses bright,
A rose, to grace her bosom white,
  The purest of that throng.
    O lily, rose, and tender eyes!
    O fragrant lips and sweet good-byes!
    Within my heart, safe from all power,
    There lives the memory of that hour!

My love, upon her bosom fair,
  Inlaid that simple rose ;
My lily, 'midst her shining hair,
Imprison'd with such thoughtful care,
  As from fine prescience flows.
    O lily, rose, and tender eyes!
    O fragrant lips and sweet good-byes!
    Within my heart, safe from all power,
    There lives the memory of that hour!

The lily drooped before the morn,
  The rose-leaves withered lay :
"'Tis thus, my love, our love we scorn,
Kiss once again ; and, all forlorn,
  Let each pursue life's way."
    O lily, rose, and tender eyes!
    Though Death hath claimed you for his prize,
    Safe from all Death, from every power,
    There lives the memory of that hour!

ON KINNOULL.

AGAIN, Kinnoull, I breathe thine air,
  In silent liberty,
Again, I drop the mask of care,
  And stand confessed to thee!

Who, hath he love of native land,
  And heart of true-born Scot,
Can on thy noble summit stand,
  Nor glow in heart and thought?

Forgive the tears that silent steal
  Down this reproachful cheek,
Nor deem it weakness they reveal
  ' The thoughts that utterance seek.

As this fair scene I view below,
  And raise mine eyes above—
Kind Heaven, that utterance fit bestow
  Which may express my love!

Express the love I bear to thee,
  To land of home and birth,
My love for love, for liberty,
  For beauty, and for worth!

I feel a beating of the heart,
  A tightening of the hand,
A thousand quick emotions start,
  At sight of thee, dear land!

Control me, O thou spirit fine
  That permeat'st this scene!
From every earthliness refine,
  And free from all that's mean.

Make worthy thee, more true to love,
  Susceptible and kind,

The soul that longs to rise above
   The faults of heart and mind !

And thou, Kinnoull, enhallowed spot,
   Round which heart-tendrils twine,
Still let me cherish thee in thought,
   And ne'er shall I repine.

There is an influence flows from thee
   Thy child shall ne'er disown—
From thee my love of liberty,
   Of land, of love, have grown !

WORDS, WORDS.

WEAK, weak the words that greet thine ear,
   The forms that meet thy sight ;
Beneath them all, my dear, my dear,
   Oh, read my love aright !
I stretch out yearning hands to thee
   Through mist of blinding tears,
But let not these mine utterance be,
   If nothing more appears :
Sweet words may linger on the tongue,
   And tears forever flow,
Yet will true love remain unsung,
   And none its meaning know.

What love have we within our heart,
   That is a love indeed,
Can find in words a fitting part,
   Or voice in time of need ?
The shadows of this summer day
   May swiftly come and go—

What of the fervid sun have they?
  They do but mock his glow.
Take, take these words, these tears of mine—
  Oh, weak indeed am I
To scorn all words, and still to pine
  To move thee with a sigh!

I scorn the lilies in thy hair
  But now I gave to thee—
These roses that delight the air
  Are feeble mockery ;
The heaven, the earth, the running stream,
  This balmy summer air,
The glories of the sun that gleam
  And brighten everywhere—
Beseech thee, dear one, do not take
  As fitting words of love !
The shadows freeze within the brake,
  While burns the sun above.

Nay, nay, my love, I cannot pause—
  Forgive the froward love
That would convince thee of its laws,
  And be all law above.
The silences within my breast
  Are deeper than all speech—
Thou hearest words, but ah, the rest
  Doth scorn my longing reach.
This lingering kiss, this fond embrace,
  These words, these tears and sighs—
To silence let them all give place,
  For silence never lies !

LOVE'S MYSTERY.

THERE is a mystery in love
   Which oft enchains my thought,
That we should prize all else above
   Whate'er is dearly bought ;
And what we know is ours alone
We scarcely think it worth to own.

I see my love, with beaming eye,
   Come tripping o'er the lea,
I clasp her to me with a sigh
   Of silent ectasy !—
A moment more, the rapture's gone,
Our bark is launched, the stream glides on.

I kiss my love, and say good-bye,—
   Then cometh longing deep :
For what was all my own, I sigh,
   Yet would not with me keep.
The shadow of my love remains,
Rebukes my tears and mocks my pains.

Within my heart I love but one,
   And, whether far or near,
The springings of my being run
   From her, my love, my dear ;
Yet, when afar she seemeth near,
And, present, distant doth appear.

The wherefore love so strange should be,
   A mystery remains,
If it be not that, distant, we
   Behold what, nearer, pains :
We know our hands must shield our eyes
When gazing at the noon-day skies.

TWA AULD FOUK.

THERE'S twa auld fouk I lo'e richt weel,
    An' twa auld fouk lo'e me,
Twa hairts I ken are kind an' leal,
    Whate'er the lave may be ;
Twa heids weel straiked wi' carefu' grey,
    That think for me an' mine,
Twa pair o' een that mony a day
    Grat sair for me langsyne.
        O douce auld fouk, O dear auld fouk,
            Hoo could I've dune withoot ye ?
        I kenna if to lauch or greet
            As noo I sing aboot ye.

It's faither, mither,—ye're the twa
    That to my hairt are dear,
An' mony a nicht, tho' far awa',
    In thocht I see ye near.
There's no a breath o' caller air
    That blaws frae hameward airt
But brings fond memories to my min',
    Kind feelin's to my hairt !
        O douce auld fouk, O dear auld fouk,
            Hoo could I've dune withoot ye ?
        I kenna if to lauch or greet
            As noo I sing aboot ye.

Doon, doon the years, sae swiftly flown,
    I see ye baith again,
'Fore heids an' hairts had weary grown
    Wi' carefu' thocht an' pain.
I hear ye singin' at my bed,
    An' greet, I kenna hoo,
I feel your han's upo' my heid,
    Your kisses on my mou'.

O douce auld fouk, O dear auld fouk,
    Hoo could I've dune withoot ye?
I kenna if to lauch or greet
    As noo I sing aboot ye.

I see ye strugglin' thro' the years
    To keep us snod an' braw,
I see the saut, saut burnin' tears
    Frae weary een doonfa'.
It's late an' ear' ye're up an' doon,
    For bairns that gi'e nae heed ;
While a' the warl' is sleepin' soon',
    Ye're toilin' for oor bread.
        O douce auld fouk, O dear auld fouk,
            Hoo could we've dune withoot ye?
        I kenna if to lauch or greet
            As noo I sing aboot ye.

But little kent ye, whan ye thocht
    Us a' in slumbers deep,
The little min's that wrocht an' wrocht,
    An', thinkin', couldna sleep.
It's faither this, an' mither that,
    For us work nicht an' day—
Oh, whan we're men an' women, what
    For them will we no dae !
        O douce auld fouk, O dear auld fouk,
            Hoo could we've dune withoot ye?
        I kenna if to lauch or greet
            As noo I sing aboot ye.

An' noo, an' noo, ye're auld an' grey,
    An' in the gloamin' licht,
An' tho' it's little to gi'e we ha'e,
    Ye're welcome to it the nicht.
An' may ye live until ye dee !
    An' whan ye dee, gae whaur

There's nocht to frichten you or me,
  Or than this warl' waur!
    O douce auld fouk, O dear auld fouk,
      Hoo could I've dune withoot ye?
    I kenna if to lauch or greet
      As noo I sing aboot ye.

SUMMER LONGINGS.

OH for the scent of the heather,
  The spring of the turf 'neath my feet,
For a glimpse of the shaggy brown mountains,
  And the sound of some rivulet sweet!
For a whiff of the health-giving breezes
  That wander o'er mountain and dale—
For one hour of the pleasure of living,
  Where no trouble of life can assail!

With the clasp or a hand love-responsive,
  And a heart in accord with my own
To the music of Nature around us,
  Where love is the sweet monotone.
Oh, to wander away from thought-shadows,
  Away from the turbulent strife
Which the world in its dreaming calls being,
  And knows not the dreaming of life.

See, the bright smiling face of Dame Nature,
  Who loveth her children all,
And upraiseth to nobler stature
  The hearts on her helping that call!
Away, love, with me from the phantoms
  That track us in life's brightest day,
, To the fountain of living and loving—
  To Nature herself, let's away!

KETTINS.

SERENE, sequestered, and supremely sweet,
For dreamy poet's habitation meet ;
In tender beauty, peacefulness, and ease,
With softly-murmuring stream and whispering trees ;
Where lovely Spring, delighted, lavish showers,
In bright confusion, all her choicest flowers ;
Where rose-crowned Summer, Nature's peerless queen,
With flower-embroidered robe of emerald green,
In soft retirement loves her court to hold,
Till Autumn, king magnificent and bold,
Appears in splendrous pomp to mount his throne,
And claim fair Summer's subjects for his own ;
Where Winter, with a pure and careful hand,
His snowy mantle stretches o'er the land,
As if instructed by the seasons three—
Whose will is his, and faithful servant he—
To guard with care and jealously conceal .
The secret beauties they alone reveal :—
Fair Kettins ! Nature hath bestowed on thee
Such gifts as only for her favourite be !
Thou rustic beauty, shy and full of grace,
With look of simple wonder on thy face,
We gaze on thee, and own with happy sigh,
The beautiful alone can never die !
So much in us, so much, alas, impure,
Doth cling rebellious, doth so long endure,—
Within the presence of such suasive power
As thine, we feel thou canst new grace endower
Upon our struggling souls, new strength impart
To weakly-wavering thought and fainting heart.
Here in conception, is fit training-place
For mental athlete ere he run life's race ;
Here should all maids be fair, and men be strong
To battle for the right and conquer wrong ;

Beneath the shelter of thy peaceful bowers,
Where slow, unmarked, move on the placid hours—
Where Nature doth her lovely face disclose
From rosy morn till evening's dewy close,—
Are found the springs of life, the wells of thought,
By vain, deluded mortals elsewhere sought:
The steady centre in the wheel of life,
The soul sustentive of its toil and strife,
In which men chase the shadows of the day,
And let the seeming, for the real, sway.
As from the deep mysterious realms of night
Flash forth the glories of the morning light;
From thundrous-still eternal silence, start
The words divine that quicken mankind's heart:
So, deeper than all form, and sight, and sound—
Life's cares monotonous, the dreary round
Of sweet frivolities and vapid joys,
There moves a hand, there speaks a still small voice,
That plans and guides our thoughts and doings right,
Though nothing thus appear to mortal sight;
And through such subtlety of grace as thine
Spring swift accomplishments, by hand divine,
Of fuller, sweeter purposes than man,
With all his intellect, can grasp or scan.

Long be it thine to nurture and to train
A pure nobility, true ends to gain!
And joy to him who thinks and feels for all,
Even as his Lord, who careth for the fall
Of simple sparrow and quick-fading flower,
And firm upholdeth all with loving power:—
Like, in his sphere, his thoughtfulness and care,
If not on earth reward—'tis sure elsewhere.
And they whose lot it is to hold the land
Which God hath given with overflowing hand,
Maintain, with fitting dignity and worth,
The grace and honour of their place and birth;

Forgetting not those gracious words of Heaven,
" Thrice-blessed he who to the poor hath given ;"
While they remember, of a humbler sphere,
Our treasure is in heaven above, not here.
Such, Kettins, be thy lot.   Thou art so fair,
Let sweet consistency breathe everywhere—
Kind hearts and noble deeds with Nature's gifts
    abound—
The True, the Beautiful, and Good, in one bright
    round !

T R I F L E S.

TRIFLES, trifles, light as air,
  Make life's daily round,
By a cord of gossamer hair
  Are our beings bound :
Tears drop idly in the dust,
What we will is what we must.

Trifles, trifles mock the hand
  That would thrust aside,
Mock the voice that would command,
  Heart that would deride :
Sighs are spent upon the air,
All our efforts are despair.

Clasp me not too close, O earth,
  With presuming grace ;
Thou may'st give the body birth,
  Soul hath purer race :
Trifle thou—we need not fear,
Since our being is not here.

REPROACHFUL.

THOUGH sorrow wound with tender love,
  Hearts oft are piercéd through,
And flowers are broken on the stem
  For very weight of dew.
      How slow
  Of pace is tearful woe!
      How soon
  Our pleasures fleet away!
We think, my dear, it scarcely noon,
  When, lo, 'tis close of day.

Not every longing heart is bless'd
  With kiss for every sigh,
And willows woo the stream that runs
  In careless beauty by.
      How still
  And calm lie vale and hill!
      In vain
  For rain the workers call;
While, far upon the heedless main,
  The precious showers down fall.

Yet, though I own a happier fate,
  Since thou hast smiled on me,
The very thought thou canst be kind
  Destroys felicity.
      Ah, me,
  The hearts that sigh for thee!
      To win
  Thee, dear, who may but try?
Then think it not such grievous sin
  If I, too, sometimes sigh.

For, darling mine, thy love is more
  Than words shall speak for me;

I cannot live without I love,
I cannot love but thee.
Forget
That e'er a tear hath wet
Thy cheek,
Or thou hast sighed, for me :
Remember, love, my joy I seek
And find in loving thee.

I CANNOT TELL.

I CANNOT tell, I cannot tell
How it could ever be
That lips like thine should e'er touch mine,
Or thou shouldst smile on me.
Nay, nay,
Thou vision fair, away !
Such bliss
Was never meant for me :
Yet, dearest love, both smile and kiss
Have I received from thee.

Oh, Spring hath never breathed so sweet
As thou hast breathed on me ;
The sparkling eyes of dewy morn
Are not so fair to see
As thine,
That full on me now shine,
Dear love,
With tenderness aglow,
As I behold thee bend above,
And smile on me below.

Bend down, bend down thy fragrant lips,
Thine arms around me twine,

And quench the thirsting of my heart
  In one love-quaff divine!
      Heart-grief
Doth seldom find relief,
      Heart-bliss
But seldom lingereth long;
Come, tune my lips with one sweet kiss,
  As guerdon of my song.

I cannot tell—I cannot tell
  How it could ever be
That thy sweet lips should e'er touch mine,
  Or thou shouldst smile on me!
      Sweetheart,
I will we never part
      Till death
Shall break the golden chain
That binds our lives, or chill the breath
  Of one of us, or twain.

STAY, SPRING.

Dull winter, haste away,
Sweet springtime, ever stay;
Up, dear lark, and sing in heaven,
Through yon cloud by sunlight riven,
    Beyond the blue,
    The beautiful, the true,
Mount, lark, to thee to mount is given!

Dull winter, haste away,
Sweet springtime, ever stay;
Stay forever in my heart,
Friends are we, why should we part?
    Till thou appear,
    How dark the earth, how drear!
Stay, spring, life of the year thou art!

THE BARON AND THE MAID.

"COME, be my love," the baron cried,
    Unto the maiden fair;
"There's not a lady in the land
    Shall with my bride compare.

"For all I have shall be her own,
    No air of heaven more free,
And he shall be her slave who yet
    Hath never bent the knee."

The maiden turned her head away,
    And tearfully did sigh:
"Thou canst not win a heart that's won,"
    Was all she made reply.

"But I shall be thy husband dear,
    And faithful love also,
Thou shalt not lack a trusty knight
    Wherever thou dost go.

"A trusty arm to fend thy steps,
    And ward thee from all harm;
No trouble shall discomfort thee,
    Or fearful thoughts alarm."

The maiden looked with wistful gaze,
    And still she did but sigh:
"The heart is fixed that once hath loved,
    For love can never die."

"Then is my heart so fixed on thee!"
    The baron answered bold,
"And thou shalt surely list to me,
    Nor turn away thus cold.

"Thou knowest not the heart that seeks
    To win a smile from thee,

Nor all that he can give his love,
    If thou his love but be."

Again the maiden turned away,
    And silently did weep ;
'Twas for her love in battle slain
    That she her tryst did keep.

" Mourn not thy love," the baron cried,
    " And lift thy drooping head !
See'st not, sweetheart, 'tis he himself,
    Returnéd from the dead !"

She gazed—it was her love, indeed,
    Who stood with smiling face—
A moment wavers she in doubt,
    Then sinks in his embrace !

In love, fair maids, in love be true,
    For love is all in vain
That doth not of itself reward,
    And be its own sweet gain.

SING, HAPPY BIRD.

SING, happy bird, upon yon bough,
To listening mate thou singest now,
    And ever the self-same song ;
Strange, as thou fondly o'er and o'er
Dost con thy phrasing, we the more
    For thy sweet singing long !

So would I be, sweet bird, like thee,
One theme alone sufficing me—
    One theme all themes above ;
Fain would I have my simple song
Beget in other hearts a strong
    And simple faith in love !

THE AULD CARLE AN' THE YOUNG ANE.

Och ay! an' fat are ye daein' here, young man,
    An' fat are ye daein' here?
Hoot toots! I'm lookin' for rasps, auld man,
    It's gettin' the time o' year.

Your rasps maun be gey green, young man,
    That story 'ill haurdly dae!
Weel, weel, I'll juist gae hame, auld man,
    An' come some ither day.

An' fa ever heard o' rasps, young man,
    To grow inside a hoose?
Ye're surely no o' thae pairts, young man,
    Or ha'e ither thochts, I jalooze.

Weel, gin ye are dootfu' o' me, auld man,
    Juist at your dochter speir ;
An' tho' the rasps are green, auld man,
    Your dochter's here a' the year!

Och ay! an' that's your rasps, young man,
    My lassie's bonnie mou'?
Aweel, gin she consents, young man,
    I needna object, I trew!

Weel, gin ye dinna object, auld man,
    I'll ask my lassie oot,
An' tho' the rasps are green, auld man,
    She'll mak' it up, nae doot.

For een has she like slaes, auld man,
    Like cherries her wee bit mou',
An' like twa reid, reid apples, auld man,
    Her bonnie cheeks in hue.

Wi' this an' that I'll dae, auld man,
    An' ither sweets forbye,
An' muckle obleeged to ye, auld man,
    For sic a lass am I !

O, THE HOLLY.

CHRISTMAS SONG.

I.

O, THE Holly, the bright green Holly—
What spring flower can match thee, Holly?
Beloved art thou by great and small,
A place hast thou in cot and hall ;
Thy glistening leaves and berry red
Reminding us of thorn-crowned Head—
    Oh, dearly we love thee, Holly!

II.

O, the Holly, the bright green Holly—
Emblem thou of youth's sweet folly !
Around our hearts thy leaves entwine
With many a love and memory fine ;
Oh, bring us back those days of yore,
The loved ones lost do thou restore !—
    Those merry merry days, dear Holly !

III.

O, the Holly, the bright green Holly—
Keep us all from melancholy !
The joys we crave are not of earth—
Our hearts imbue with heavenly mirth ;
And while thy leaves hang on our wall,
Oh, may they nought but joy recall,
    For dearly we love thee, Holly !

on page 63.

HARMONY.

COME, love, and while we wander free,
Some questionings I will put to thee :
What says the lark that greets the morn,
On fluttering wings of song upborne ?
   " I love, I love," is all his song,
   " To love alone these notes belong ! "

What says the sun at hot noontide,   ·
All-amorous clasping earth, his bride ?
What say the flowers that find their birth,
Upon the breast of blushing earth ?
   " We love, we love," they answering call,
   " 'Tis love begets and stays us all ! "   ·

What say the brook that ripples by,
And freshening raindrops from the sky ?
The stars that watch the earth asleep,
The dawn that on the night doth creep ?
   " We love, we love," quick answer they,
   " No law but love can we obey."

And how shall tender-hearted youth,
Who, if he speak, must speak the truth,
Refuse to swell the thrilling strain,
In hope 'twill echo back again ?
   I love, I love, and love but thee—
   Sweet, answer thou—thou lovest me !

COMFORT-KNOWLEDGE.

THERE is a comfort none may know
But they who tread the paths of woe ;
This comfort-knowledge them is given—
The paths of grief are paths to heaven.

ONE STAR.

ONE star above, one face below,
One light of love on both, I trow,—
One lingering, quivering hope beyond
The longings of a heart too fond,
　　Too fond, O love, of thee !

Why wearily watcheth yonder star
Until the morn his gates unbar,
And Phœbus mounts the rolling skies,
With flying locks and flaming eyes—
　　Why wearily watcheth she ?

Star, quivering, straining longing eyes
To see thy lover bold arise,—
Thy longing doth true love defeat,
Thou, too, shalt pale to know the cheat
　　Of loving foolishly !

Turn, Star, thy gaze to dullard earth !
Behold how mortals slight their birth,
Stretch out presuming arms of love
To heavens of happiness above
　　The powers the fates decree !

Beam on us, Star, with radiance free,
'Tis we who love thee reverently ;
Let Phœbus pass with melting scorn,
Thou never shalt for love be lorn
　　While we thy beaming see !

Thus, thus—a patient gives the cure
For ills he fain would still endure :
Show me some perfect way, sweet Star,
To crush the longings that would mar
　　The growth of love in me !

ROSE SCENT.

ALL through the silent night,
  With one sweet-smelling rose
    Which my dear love has given,
I sit in tranced delight,
  Until the morning glows,
    And the lark sings in his heaven.

The breathing of that flower
  Waves through my pulsing soul
   . With motions never-ending ;
I feel its subtle power,
  Its secret strong control,
    My willings heavenward bending.

And all the more I maze,
  In wandering, wildering quest,
    For meaning of rose-breathing,
And all the more I gaze
  Upon my love's bequest,
    With thought in thought enwreathing,—

I weave the air in vain :
  For, though the earth is ours,
    And heaven our hope before us,
The mystery doth remain,
  To baffle all our powers,
    Within, around, and o'er us.

Breathe on, heaven-odorous rose,
  That fillest my ravished soul
    With dreams of things forgotten !
Heaven only may disclose
  Why thus thou canst control
    These tears by thee begotten.

THE DYING STREET SINGER.

WELL, Moll, my time is nearly up,
  And all I've got to say,
Is, trudge along to yonder town,
  And leave me by the way.
It ain't no use, I tell thee, Moll,
  To bother any more—
Before the morning dawns again,
  I know 'twill all be o'er.
So, trudge along, my darling lass,
  And leave me here behind,
I couldn't stir a blessed peg,
  Though all the world were kind.

And *thou*'st been kind, I trow thee, lass,
  And not too kind been I—
What, kinder than thyself, say'st thou?
  Nay, Molly, don't thee cry!
Ain't thou my dear?   Let's grip thy hand :
  Well, 'tis some years ago
Since first it trembled in my own—
  I loved thee then, I know.
And maybe, Moll, have loved thee since,
  Though not so plain to see
As all the tenderness and care
  Which thou bestowed on me.

But when we lost our little all,
  And things from bad grew worse—
I think the love within me turned
  A blessing to a curse.
Oh, Molly, Molly! kiss thy lad,
  Who'll never stir again—
'Twas many a time wild love of thee
  That made me give thee pain!
To see thee trudge through rain and snow,

Through miles and miles of street,
With scarce a rag to cover thy back,
  Or shoes for thy poor feet:
To hear thee singing at my side,
  And know 'twas love of me
That made thee stand the gibes and sneers
  Of cruel humanity—
Forgive me, Molly! 'twas too much,
  Too much for such as me!
I cursed the very love you had,
  Yet would have died for thee.
And here, all in a common ditch,
  I've tumbled down to die,
While you're a-shivering there with cold,
  And not a coin have I.
And not a blessed bite or sup
  You've had this weary day——
Keep that 'ere shawl upon your back,
  And, hark ye, get away!
Away, away, too faithful lass,
  That ever could be kind
To such a wretched cur as I,
  That now must lag behind!

Why ain't thee going, Moll, I say?
  Dost see the stars are bright,
And don't thee feel the biting frost,
  This cruel winter night?
Thou'lt never leave me, sayest thou?
  Wouldst die, indeed, for me?
Nay, needless, Moll; but let me put
  My head upon thy knee.
The cold? Not I, dear lass, not I;
  Here, take this old coat off,
And put it 'cross thy shoulders: there,
  And don't thee mind this cough.

*   *   *   *   *

Ah! 'tis a lovely eve in June—
  I hear the blackbirds sing
Down by the brimming river,
  Where tender willows swing.
And thou and I are wandering on,
  Thy hand, sweet Moll, in mine;
What's all the world to thee and me,
  If love our hearts entwine?
Just see that sun sink glorious,
  All in the glowing west!
Now, isn't that a sight, my dear,
  To fill each grateful breast?
Here, 'neath this honeysuckle sweet,
  We'll seat us side by side;
To-morrow will be a happy day,
  For thou shalt be my bride,
And I thy tender husband true—
  Two hearts in loving strong——

    *   *   *   *   *

Eh, dreaming, say'st thou?   Where are we?
  The road seems dark and long;
What makes thee cry, my darling lass—
  Got any meat to-day?
Let's start and sing them "Home, sweet Home,"
  And then we'll go away.
Not sing a note?   Well, never mind,
  Let me just make a try——
Ah!—Moll!—quick, raise me, dear—
  Good-bye—sweetheart—good—bye!

STREAM, STREAM.

STREAM, stream, run to the sea,
Run to thy love who is waiting thee,
    With bosom calm and deep :
Love, love, haste thou to me,
Here to this bosom, oh, let me clasp thee,
    And there forever keep.

Droop, droop, willow love-lorn,
Over the stream that runs past thee in scorn,
    The stream that seeks the sea :
Love, love, scorn not my plaint,
Succour thy lover despairing and faint,
    Look tenderly on me.

Fall, fall, heavenly rain, fall
Into the stream that engulfeth all,
    The cruel, glittering stream :
Love, love, see my tears flow,
Heed them, my dearest, and comfort bestow,
    Of hope but grant one gleam.

Sink, sink, sun of the west,
Thou hast a longing like man for thy rest,
    The stream doth seek the sea :
Love, love, hear my sad cry,
Save me despairing and longing to die,
    Forsake, forsake not me.

CHILD-HEART.

As a child, as a child, let me feel,
    And act, and think, and speak,
With the gift, as a child, to reveal,
    The truths men vainly seek.

SLICHTED.

Oh, but my heid is low,
  An', oh, my hairt is sair,
There's nocht on a' the earth
  To comfort ony mair.

My hairt, my hairt will brak,
  An' ye ha'e dune it, Johnny ;
What comfort is't to ken
  My face ye aince thocht bonnie ?

Oh, mither, dinna greet,
  But kiss your bairn again,
I wish the tears wad come,
  That canna come for pain.

Oh, faither, dinna flyte,
  It's little did I dree
That I sud see the day
  Ye baith wad turn frae me.

Turn frae your bonnie bairn,
  Wha thochtna to dae wrang,
Wha's heid is bowed wi' shame,
  Wha winna hin'er lang.

Oh, mither, bonnie mither,
  Juist kiss me aince again :
I wish I was your lassie,
  As in the days bygane.

I wish it was the simmer,
  An' I could rin an' play,
Rin oot an' meet my faither
  Come in at close o' day.

Come in an' kiss his dawtie,
   An' tak' me on his knee,
An' straik my gowden ringlets,
   An' sing to me wi' glee.

" Ye'll be a bonnie lassie,
   Ye'll be a bonnie dear,
Ye'll no ha'e want o' laddies,
   Although no fash'd wi' gear."

Oh that my hairt wad brak,
   Or that I could but greet,
Or that I could forgat
   Thae memories sae sweet.

An' I ha'e dune it a',
   Ha'e brocht ye a' your grievin',
An' yet I canna greet,
   Though pain my hairt is reivin'.

Upon my weary bed
   Juist lay me doon the nicht,
I carena tho' I dee
   Afore the mornin' licht.

Oh, Johnny, Johnny lad,
   I lo'ed ye owre weel,
I little thocht ye'd wrang
   Your lass sae true an' leal.

Oh, ha'e a thocht o' her,
   Whan she has gane awa',
Wha lo'ed ye to her shame,
   An' ye were fause for a'.

MILLER, MILLER.

I.

MILLER, miller, dusty-white,
    Let thy mill go round,
There is pleasure in the sight,
    Music in the sound.
        Let the waters rush,
        Let the millstones crush
Mellow gliding golden grain,
        While my love, a-blush,
Runs to meet her love again !

Miller, miller, dusty-white,
    'Tis a weary year
Since the mill last filled my sight,
    Whirred upon my ear.
        Let the wheel go round,
        Merry is the sound,
Waking hopes and memories sweet,
        While my love doth bound
Forward her true love to greet.

II.

Miller, miller, dusty-white,
    What is that thou weep'st !—
Say not that I hear aright,
    That my maiden sleeps !
        O thou dreadful mill,
        Grinding, grinding still,
While my love lies 'neath the clay !
        Me, too, do thou kill,
If I near thee longer stay !

Miller, miller, dusty-white,
    Though thy mill go round,

There is mocking in the sight,
Horror in the sound.
Let the waters rush,
Let the millstones crush
Hearts and hopes for golden grain—
O my love, a-hush,
Thou shalt never come again !

MARIE.

SHE sits in owre her carriage braw,
An' looks as though she ne'er had seen
Young Davie wha she kiss'd yestreen
Doon in yon bonny birken shaw.

Oh, 'twas a leddy fine an' fair,
Wi' routh o' gear, wi' high degree,
Wha for her simple lad wad dee,
An' ocht that love sud, for him dare ;

A leddy's faither, glum and dour,
Wha couldna min' the days he lo'ed,
An' his ain lassie's mither wooed,
An' thocht the warl' beside her puir ;

An', syne, a lad wha lo'ed a lass,
An' hadna but his plaid to share ;
Yet, couldna will to lat her dare
What she micht smile at an' lat pass.

Young Davie cried, "Gae 'wa, Marie,
An' hie ye to yon bonnie ha'
Whaur ye are queen an' pride o' a',
An' lat your lad gae owre the sea."

" An' I'll gae wi' ye, laddie true,"
  The halesome lassie cried ootricht :
  " The mornin' comes, an' wi' it licht,
Sae, lat us baith mak' aff the noo !"

" I'll ha'e nae love, my leddy fair,
  That isna a' my ain by richt ;
  Gin ye will gae wi' me the nicht,
We'll to your faither's ha' repair !"

The faither straik his auld grey beard,
  An' keekit 'neath his lowerin' broo :
  " Weel, gin ye think ye're no to rue,
This very nicht ye twa'll be paired !"

The lassie lauched an' grat wi' glee,
  Her cheeks like roses wat wi' dew,
  While Davie aff his plaidie threw,
An' stood a knicht o' fair degree !

Weel micht she won'erin' stan' an' stare,
  He clasps her in his lovin' arms ;
  " Ye're a' my ain, an' love's alarms
Sall your fond hairt disturb nae mair !"

The faither lauchs as he wad dee :
  " Ech, lassie, ye're a thrawsome thing !
  Ye wadna tak' the waddin' ring
That noo ye beg on bended knee !

" Rise up, my bonnie, bonnie dear,
  Your cousin is the lad ye lo'e,
  'An' gin ye'd lat your cousin woo,
Ye'd nocht, ye see, frae him to fear !"

A FACE.

It was a face of sweetness,
  That gazed in mine
  In the pale moonshine,
Complete with love's completeness.

Art thou my heart not nearest?
  The pale moon high
  For morn doth sigh
As I for thee, my dearest!

It was a face of sweetness
  That said me nay,
  And turned away,
But not with love's completeness.

The moon above was shining:
  My heart went out
  In throbbing doubt
As there I stood repining.

O moon, thou art forsaken,
  And waitest on
  Until by dawn,
Thy fickle love, o'ertaken!

Shall I, for love returning,
  Wait till the morn
  With heart forlorn,
Or give all loving spurning?

Love-maiden, yonder beaming—
  Nor thou nor I   .
  Can but reply,
Save love, all else is seeming.

Return, my face of sweetness!
  For thee I long,
  With needings strong—
In thee I find completeness!

DUETTO PASTORALE.

ILLA.

Languemente.

How I wish my lot were cast
  In some silent forest vast,
Where no sounds of toil or strife
  Should disturb my simple life !
There, from care and thinking free,
  All the world were nought to me ;
Singing all the happy day,
  Till kind death should still my lay :
Daily thought and nightly dream
  Have but one recurring theme—
How I wish, oh, how I pray,
  I could wander far away,
                All alone !

ILLE.

Giocoso.

'Tis a mystery that in vain
  I have striven to explain,
But, to me, how oft have come
  Longings for just such a home !
I'm awearied with the strife
  And the trouble of this life :
Wonder if there's such a spot
  Where one might have happier lot ?
Wonder what I'd think or do,
  Were I separate from you ?
On reflection—don't quite care
  For sojourning anywhere
                All alone !

Amoroso.

  Come, now dearest—what think you ?

If you go, let me go, too ;
Don't you, now, in tender mood,
    Sometimes think a mate were good ?
Or, if that unwelcome be—
    Come along, my dear, with me !
Both our paths are quite the same,
    Differing now but in a name—
That is much the better way,
    To my thinking, than to say,
                        "All alone !"

Agitato.

Quickly tell me—"yes" or "no,"
    Will you come, or will I go ?
Here, impatient, do I stand,
    Ready for that vision land ;
But, ah me, how well I know
    Joy is only where you go !
Never shall I find the heart
    From delights of love to part—
Darling, answer "yes" or "no,"—
    Answer not that you will go
                        All alone !

Con dolce concento.

Down upon my heaving breast
    Dropped a head in tranquil rest,
Up there turned a happy face,
    Full of confidence and grace :
"Take me, dear ; I do not know
    Path untrodden thou may'st go ;
Care not for the sighs and tears
    May await the coming years :
Yet, I'd rather go astray,
    Love, with you, than take my way
                        All alone !"

A DROP OF INK.

A DROP of ink
                In rhymes
May make words clink
                At times,
With gracefulness and ease
That sight and hearing please,
                Without
The slightest doubt ;
                And yet,
May ne'er beget
                A thought
                Worth aught
But to forget
That one could ever think
Of a little drop of ink.

I'll run my ink
                In rhymes,
And make words clink
                At times
With what they can of ease,
The eye and ear to please,
                Without
Arousing doubt ;
                And yet
Hope they beget
                A thought
                Worth aught
But to forget
That any one could think
By a little drop of ink.

Thou drop of ink !
                In rhymes

Go forth, and clink
　　The times
From inward treacherous ease,
And poor deceits that please
　　Without,
　To healthful doubt ;
　　And yet,
　In hearts beget
　　　Some thought
　　　Worth aught
　But to forget :
For men may feel and think
By thee, thou drop of ink !

　O drop of ink!
　　In rhymes
Smooth words may clink
　　At times
With unavailing ease
If sense alone they please,
　　Without
　The slightest doubt ;
　　And yet,
　I would beget
　　　One thought
　　　Worth aught
　But to forget—
That heaven itself may blink
In a little drop of ink !

YOUNG GILBERT.

BESIDE the little trysting stile,
　　Endeared by many a vow,
Young Gilbert, from across the seas,
　　Awaits sweet Marion now.

"Come quickly, love, the moon is high,
　　And my heart is wild to-night
For a touch of thy lips and a look of thy face,
　　Upturn'd in the sweet moonlight.

"Upturn'd and wet, but not with the tears
　　Thou shed'st that night long ago
When around me thy dear arms were thrown,
　　And my heart was loth to go.

"Come running, my love, with tears of joy,
　　And welcoming arms outspread,
　How many days and nights have I longed
　　For that rest to my weary head!

"Speed, speed, my dear!　My eager heart
　　Will burst ere I clasp you again,
Ere I feel the touch of your hand on my brow
　　Becalming its throbbing pain.

"Oh, long and sadly I've striven and toiled
　　Since last I saw you here,
With aching heart and wearied hand,
　　And all for thee, my dear;

"But now I come with tidings glad—
　　Haste, haste, my love to hear—
I have wealth, I have wealth, and the prize is
　　　won
　　I have fought for many a year!

"And how I shall laugh at your wondering look
As I show you all that's thine!
The dreary past shall be as a dream,
As I clasp thy dear heart to mine!"

A stranger came, and led him where
His love lay still and cold,
A look of wonder on her face
At things he had not told.

A wreath of lilies on her brow,
'Twas fair as they were fair;
Her hands upon her bosom clasp'd
As if in silent prayer.

He cast one strange, one passionate look
Upon that upturn'd face,
His arms he threw around that form
In one long last embrace;

One kiss upon those cold, cold cheeks,
That once were roses sweet,
One smothered sob of a broken heart,
And heaven beheld them meet.

———⚬⚔⚬———

PIQUE.

NOT a look, not a sigh,
Not a tender-sweet good-bye?
      Parting is but sorrow!
Not a clasping, not a kiss?
Must we part, my love, like this?
      Love again to-morrow!

Love thou art, love shalt be
Ever mine, as I to thee—
      Lovers we forever!
Morn is hasting up the sky,
Will thee, nil thee, love, good-bye,
      Till the night we sever!

IT'S A' OWRE.

IT'S a' owre, it's a' owre,
　　She gaed last nicht at ten,
Come in, guid neebours, come awa',
　　An' lat me tak' ye ben.
Ye see, she's sleepin' soon'er noo
　　Than last ye cam' to speir,
She's quiet eneuch, the bonnie doo,
　　She'll wauk nae mair, the dear!

Oh, ay; she spak' na muckle o't,
　　An' tho' she suffered sair,
Ye never heard her mak' complaint,
　　Except, maybe, in prayer.
For whan she thochtna we were by,
　　She'd aften sab an' greet,
An' eh, 'twas pitifu' to hear
　　Her tearfu' voice sae sweet!

Na, na; he never cam' ava,
　　Tho' aft he would, she said,
An' ilka stap upo' the stairs
　　Would mak' her lift her heid.
An' then she'd clasp her wee bit han's,
　　An' glowre wi' startin' een,
Until the door was opened wide,
　　An' unkent faces seen.

Then doon upo' her pillow white
　　She'd fa' wi' weary sigh,
The tear-draps tricklin' frae her een,
　　That scarce were ever dry.
Owre to the wa' she'd turn her face,
　　An' greet till sleep would come,
An' tho' I tried to comfort her,
　　I micht as weel been dumb.

Ay, but she was a bonnie lass,
  An' kind an' leal forbye,
An' tho' she may ha'e dune some wrang,
  'Twas no her blame, say I.
O laddie, laddie, whaur ye be
  I dinna ken or care,
But muckle is the doot in me
  Gin ye ha'e acted fair.

Eh? tak' a payment, did ye say?
  Na, na; I'm weel content
To keep this bonnie locket, slipt
  Aneath her heid unkent.
Twa locks o' glintin' gowden hair,
  In lovers' knottie wrocht—
Eh, but there's mony a sair, sair hairt,
  Aince kiss'd withoot a thocht!

L E A L.

GIN ye had lo'ed me, Willie,
  Wi' love but like my ain,
Ye hadna wooed me, Willie,
  Syne left me here alane.
Oh, but my hairt is riven,
  That I ha'e lo'ed ava,
But whaur true love is given,
  It's wha can tak't awa'?

Sae, dinna, dinna grieve me
  An' ask me to forgi'e,
Ye'll never mair deceive me,
  Since I am gaun frae thee.
You're surely weel forgiven
  Gin prayers are ocht for thee,
An' tho' my hairt thou'st riven,
  I'm thine eternally.

TO THE POET.

HAST thou a Poet's longings, then?
Hast thou the love that claims all men
As fellows of a common kind,
With one fine unity of mind
And secret interlinking thought,
With subtle, silent issues fraught?
Hast thou the wish to touch the heart
Of human sympathies, and start
Deep longings in the sluggish breast
That careth only for the rest
That grasps the spirit and the will
And hoarsely whispers—"Curse, be still!"
Wouldst slay the demons of the night
That come in semblance of the light?
Wouldst shoot thine arrows in the dark,
With nought to guide thee but the spark
Of solitary star above,
The solitary star of love?
Hast thou a hand to clasp thy foe,
And see divinity below
The staring vacancies of face
That mark the abasement of our race?
Hast thou a heart, a mind, a will
That must, forever, ever still
Seek out the wherefore of thy birth,
The central meaning of this earth :
That with a savage joy doth seize
The flippancies that mankind please,
And dash them with awakening shock
At forms and visages that mock
The heavenly origin and clime
Whence man, and earth, and things of time?
Dost scorn the drivelling cant of sect,
Complacent, frigid, self-elect,

That stretches finger-tips abroad
In praying patronage to God :
That knoweth all, and only knows,
Yet daily wandering further goes?
Is there a sleep abroad on all
That for thy waking cry doth call—
Doth mankind dream and think they wake,
And in their dreams the truth forsake ?
Dost thou perceive, where men are blind,
Yet barely find'st one ready mind
To seize and grapple with thy truth,
But blinking eyes instead, forsooth ?
Dost see, unseen, dost feel, unfelt,
And do thy tearful yearnings melt
In secret tenderness and care
That none perceive the Poet there?

    Utter, utter, thou man of God !
The truth reveal, the truth abroad
In scattering profusion cast—
Be it the first, and it the last !
Strike deep, with penetrating knife,
Lay bare the arteries of life,
And from lethargic sleep arouse
The spirit in its charnel-house—
The dim, benumbed, environed soul
That knows not starting-place or goal !
Flash in men's eyes the torch of heaven,
For this alone to thee 'twas given ;
Their wants ignore, and give unsought
Such joys as entered not their thought—
The dream of life explain away,
And show their night the real day,
The strugglings of this chrysalis-life
With fuller, finer, living rife—
Strike out, strike out, thou kindly foe,
There's life in every deadly blow !

O Poet, if thou hast the will,
Thou canst a glorious hope fulfill !
Behold, mankind in writhing pain
Are seeking—what ?   Thyself explain :
Their sightless eyeballs to the skies
They raise with agonising cries ;
With wringing hands and throbbing breast
They wander on some wildering quest ;
In vain the man to brother turns—
His helpless prayers he scorns and spurns,
Or in magnificence of pride,
By silence, ignorance doth hide.
What is't man seeks ?   Oh, be it now
To give the wherefore and the how,
The needed helping and the voice,
To guide men in their wavering choice !
They seek, they seek—behold it plain—
They seek to find THEMSELVES again !
They know it not, but clamouring cry
For power to live, yet haste to die ;
Their own creations make their goal—
The quivering impulses of soul
That struggle for an utterance free
They see yet know not what they see ;
There flashes on their strainèd sight
Reflections of that inward light
That speaks the deity in men,
Yet is remotest from their ken,
And glory from within that streams
Through startled rents an alien seems
To their amazèd, wandering eyes,
That turn, bewildered to the skies :
Their face within a glass they see,
Then fall in prone idolatry !

Stand forth, thou Herculean soul !
From towering, heavenly heights, down-roll

On shivering mortals' bowéd head
Thy thundering words, and from the dead
Awaken mankind into life,
And stir within them healthful strife !
Stretch forth thy sinewy hands and grasp
Life's dragging reins, and while men gasp,
And shout, and reel—away, away,
Lead on thy chariot to the day !
Tear from this suffocating race
The bondages of time and space ;
Give men the consciousness their own—
The consciousness which thou hast known :
That all they see and all they know—
The longings that forever flow
In weltering streams of love and pain,
Or dash the cheek with tearful rain :
The floating visions of the night
That flash upon their trembling sight :
The great infinities that ring
Their mental vision, wandering :
The faint perceptions of a clime
Where time was not, and yet the time
That is to come seemed in the past—
The future first, the present last :—
Are all, all, ALL the wondrous birth
Of man's abnormal state on earth !
Make men remember ; make them feel
What only thou canst e'er reveal—
That consciousness is their's alone
Who feel the universe their own !

A C R O S T I C S.

TO D. S. L.

DEVOID of poetry, wit, and sense,
Smooth rhymes afford poor recompense ;
Light is the pen that glides along
On themes like these, in weakness strong ;
With formal ease and wordy wit,
See how the rhymes and rhythms fit—
Of pen, ink, paper *quantum suff.*,
No more's required, since they're enough !

DEVOTED to the lettered arts,
So be thy will as is thy skill !
Let love, which moveth all men's hearts,
On those around like dew distill.
What gifts are thine, what noble sphere,
Such fruitful, happy fields hast thou !
Oh, may reproving thought or fear
Ne'er pain thy heart or cloud thy brow !

TO BERTIE G——.

BABY, Baby, simple, pure,
Every grace thou hast, endure :
Richest blessings from above,
Tenderest offerings of love,
Influences sweet and rare,
Earthly joy and heavenly care,
Go with thee along life's road,
Enter with thee Heaven's abode—
Eastward, to the rising sun,
Keep thee, till thy race be run :
Infant pure forever be,
Earth and Heaven alike to thee !

THE LARK.

Now, Lark, that sing'st in this sweet morning air,
   Thou hast the secret of true song!
The tender throbbings of thy spirit rare
   Beget in us the power to long—
The power to long and struggle, power to love
The world below and heaven above.

Thou leav'st a humble nest on dewy ground
   To herald in the glowing morn,
With such sweet gushings forth of tremulous sound
   As surely ne'er of earth were born ;
And, well we know, when day is done—to earth
Thou dost return, nor scorn'st thy humble birth.

Thou singest only of one theme—'tis well,
   For love alone sufficeth all,
And we who, longing 'neath thy singing, dwell,
   In love, for love, by loving, call :
Thy mounting song doth wavering hearts assure
'Tis love alone forever shall endure.

Sing out, triumphant songster of the sky !
   And from the depths of love profound
Bring forth the treasures of thy minstrelsy
   To shed, profuse, on hearts around :
As thirsty earth cool morning dews doth drink,
Deep in our hearts thy strains celestial sink.

Thy sun-struck image in this morning air,
   The throbbings of that swelling song,
Awake in us a strange, a sweet despair
   That thou couldst e'er to earth belong :
While we who walk the earth grope on in night,
Thou float'st above in realms of song and light.

Yet art thou ours, and sing'st in tones we know
  A melody that ne'er can die—
That down the eternal ages still will go
  When gone are earth, and sea, and sky:
Oh, teach us, Lark, thy song of heavenly mirth,
And while we upward mount, to sing to earth!

————o⨯⬗⨯o————

LISTEN, CHILDREN, TO THE CLOCK.

TO THE REV. J. F., *Kittms*

IN a sabbath-school I know,
Children sometimes restless grow,
Ruffling, shuffling with their feet,
Talking as if on the street;
Then the teacher lifts his hand,
Stills them with this quaint command:
" Listen, children, to the clock—
Tick—tick—tick—tock ! "

Such a hush comes over all,
One might hear a rose-leaf fall;
Boys and girls, with smiling face,
Stop their talking, keep their place.
Hold their breath, and silent sit,
Till the teacher says—" That's it !
That's the ticking of the clock—
Tick—tick—tick—tock ! "

Brethren, children older grown,
Might take lesson, were it known;
In the bustle and the strife,
And confusion of this life,
For one briefest moment stop,
Earth, with care and strivings drop,
Turn within and hear the clock—
Tick—tick—tick—tock !

SIGHS AND PRAYERS.

Oh, sigh, my dear, my dearest, sigh!
The throbbings of my bosom cry
    In helplessness to thee,
To give the utterance that is thine—
Our hearts in one faint sigh combine,
    And let it be for me.

Oh, let it not be said, my love,
While thou dost breathe to Heaven above
    Thy prayer in tender sighs,
That he who longs for thy sweet prayer
Doth give no utterance to the air,
    But on thy prayer relies:

To thee I pray, my darling one,
Thy gentle will I would be done,
    Oh, turn me not away!
Impure, unworthy all, I bow,
And plead thy pleading graces now,
    So please thee if it may!

Be thou my intercessor: I
Know not to pray but for thy sigh,
    And thou dost sigh for me;
Let not my prayer to thee be vain,
Sigh, sigh, my love, oh, sigh again,
    My soul depends on thee!

And if Heaven turn unwilling ear
To thy sweet pleadings—all is here
    A hopelessness for me;
I lift my hands, resign my will,
To Heaven I pray, my darling still—
    Pray, darling, still, for thee!

O Heaven, my love's own Heaven, be near!
The pleadings of my dear one hear—
   Not for herself prays she;
Comfort her tenderness and tears,
Her languishings and trembling fears—
   Her sighs are prayers for me!

VISIONS.

ATHWART the horizon of my soul,
   By sudden gleams of heaven lit,
Beyond faint mortals' weak control,
   Ethereal forms and fancies flit,
Athwart the horizon of my soul.

With longing arms astretch, I gasp
   And struggle to release the bands
That bind to sordid earth, and clasp
   The air; and while wave mocking hands,
With longing arms astretch, I gasp.

Remain, fair visitants to earth!
   I know, indeed, unworthy I,
Of earthly parentage and birth,
   Can only long, and pine, and sigh,
Remain, fair visitants to earth!

Yet, in some heavenly land of dreams,
   I trust there still is hope for me:
Perchance—so to my heart it seems—
   Familiar will our greetings be
Yet, in some heavenly land of dreams.

IN VAIN.

OH, take 'me, love, from love away,
   If thou dost love indeed,
These pains and agonisings, stay,
   That on my being feed :
Love, love, is not for mortals born,
It only fools us on to scorn !

Enclasp me not within those arms
   Which ope to welcome me,
Chide not these vague and faint alarms
   That cry aloud to thee :
From hearts that love tear love away,
Love is too strong for mortal clay !

Forgive my tears—'tis peaceful ease
   Love never, never gives—
Oh, tell me wherefore joys ne'er please,
   And on our griefs we live—
The sorrow gotten of our love
Is o'er our joys as heaven above !

O that my love could answer me,
   Could free me from love's bands—
O that my heart were constantly
   Accord with love's commands !
I know not which to take or leave—
The pains of love or joys that grieve.

Start from the prison of my soul—
   My language and my voice,
One moment give me love's control
   To know, to speak my choice :
Ah me, ah me ! how weak, how vain—
In love's sweet pains I sink again !

STAY, DONALD.

ARE ye awa', Donald,
   Is it guid nicht ?
Bide e'enin' fa', Donald,
   Bide mornin' licht.
Gin I spak' wrang, Donald,
   Dinna gae 'wa,
Love isna strang, Donald,
   Looks na owre a',
Come back again, Donald,
   Come to your lass,
A' that can pain, Donald,
   Lichtly lat pass ;
But bonnie love, Donald,
   Gaes on for aye,
A' words above, Donald—
   Stay, Donald, stay !

SONNET.—TO A—— R——.

NAY, friend of happy youth and days of grace,
To whom, by friendship's ever-tightening chain,
My heart, as sharer of thy joy and pain,
Is link'd in one eternal, close embrace—
Refuse the unwelcome guests to entertain,
The ghost Despondency and sombre train,
With ghoul-like wings outspread and grappling beak,
Who in the tenderest hearts their victims seek.
A sympathetic union binds our lives :
Each in his sphere with trifling trouble strives,
Each longs for strength to tread a firmer ground,
And feels the need of Heaven within, around ;
To heart, dear Alec, take this cherished thought,—
Our life is yet to come—this life is nought.

ONE LANGUAGE.

THERE'S not a breath of air,
　　There's not a drop of rain,
But hath a meaning rare,
　　But hath a meaning plain ;
There's not a simple flower,
　　A cloudlet in the sky,
But hath a subtle power,
　　A power that ne'er can die :
'Tis love they all consenting cry,
From simple flower to cloudlet high.

Come, Nature, breathe on me,
　　My wayward will control,
And, with thy sympathy,
　　Refresh my longing soul.
I would I could be pure,
　　As simple as thou art,
Could passively endure
　　To utter from the heart :
'Tis love, I know, doth work in thee,
I would 'twere always love in me !

CHOICE.

RANGE where thou wilt, my Fancy-free—
Thou hast the universe for me,
　　So love indeed be mine :
Lore, wealth, and fame may fill thy thought,
Yet all to love are nought, are nought,
　　The human to divine !

THE HUSBAND'S LITTLE PICKLE.

WELL, darling, you're not home to-night,
  Although you were expected,
I must confess I'm in a plight,
  And very much dejected ;
This bachelor's life is quite a bore,
I wish, indeed, that it were o'er.

Here's every dish set in a pile,
  So dirty, I'm disgusted ;
I've used them all in proper style,
  Until with dirt encrusted ;
So, now they're safe upon the floor,
I'll order in as many more.

And then the coals were rather low,
  So, to be economical,
I made the kitchen table go
  In pieces anatomical ;
The old piano next I'll use—
I'm sure you'll praise my thrifty views.

My hat, most strange, I couldn't find,
  Nor cuffs or shirts—no matter,
The drapers here are very kind,
  And so, indeed, each hatter ;
I've got a score of hats or more,
And shirts and cuffs a perfect store.

The weather, too, was very bad,
  The streets, in fact, were horrid,
I dirtied every boot I had—
  But, don't, my dear, be worried,
For every time the sky grew fair,
I went and bought another pair.

And, as for eatables, my dear—
  With thoughtfulness exceeding,
The grocers and the butchers here
  Have tended to my needing ;
But half-a-dozen legs of mutton
Are lying about, not worth a button.

The milk you left, I'm sorry to say,
  Got really past the using
About the sixth or seventh day—
  Although it seems amusing
That milk should not be fresh each day
As 'twas before you went away.

But now, my dear, I've struck a " bright "
  I'm sure must please you greatly,
For in the parlour, snug and tight,
  With mien and look so stately—
A nice brown cow—such sweet surprise—
Gives daily fresh and large supplies.

But, spite of all I can contrive,
  On craziness I border;
I fear, that when you do arrive,
  You'll find some slight disorder:
I really wish you were at home,
And hope you won't think more to roam.

MY BONNIE LASS FRAE TULLYMET.

'Twas on a bonnie simmer morn,
As I gaed ower the Muir o' Thorn,
I met a lass I'll ne'er forget,
Wha said she cam' frae Tullymet.
She had sic een, sic rosy mou',
Sic gowden hair and snawy broo—
Her image in my hairt is set,
That bonnie lass frae Tullymet !

She speired the way—I took her airm,
An' wi' her gaed, to 'fend frae hairm ;
The lav'rock liltin' in the sky
Was no o' lichter hairt than I.
She gaed her way, an' I gaed mine—
I've never seen my lass sin' syne ;
But never can this hairt forget
That bonnie lass frae Tullymet !

O lassie, gin ye thocht o' me
But hauf the thochts I hae o' thee,
I'd rin an' tak' ye in my arms—
My hairt's sae reived wi' love's alarms.
Ye'd never speir the way again,
Gin I had leave your ways to ten',
An' a' my houp's I'll meet you yet,
My bonnie lass frae Tullymet !

------o◈o------

SHAKESPEARE.

SHAKESPEARE ! thy name gigantic towers
Above all time and earthly powers ;
What homage can they give to thee
Who art for all eternity ?
Creator thou of realms of thought,
With such luxurious fruitage fraught,
The blossomings of our feeble day
Spring fragrant from thy nobler bay.
A halo spheres thy classic brow
That scintillates even brighter now,
Than when this earth by thee was trod—
Man simple then, but now a god !

—o◈o—

GONE AWAY.

GONE away, did you say,
  And left his poor mother?
Could not stay, did you say,
  Away from another?
Could not stay from blue eyes,
  From sweet smiles and soft fingers,
While his mother here lies,
  On her last bed here lingers?
    Gone away, gone away!
      O my son, dear son,
      I can still for thee pray
        Till my short race is run.

Not a word, did you say,
  Had no thought of his mother?
Like a bird, did you say,
  Spread wings for another?
Not a look, not a sigh,
  Not a sign of regretting,
While his mother must die
  Ere yon sun finds his setting?
    Gone away, gone away!
      O my son, dear son,
      I can still for thee pray
        Till my short race is run.

Not my own, did you say,
  Not the son of his mother?
Should disown him, you say,
  Since he loved more another?
O my son, flesh and bone!
  Thy poor mother can never
Forget thou'rt her own
  Though thou'st left her forever!
    Gone away, gone away!
      O my son, dear son,
      Thy poor mother can pray
        That the Lord's will be done!

TO ANTHEA.

A Phantasy.

COME, Anthea, beauteous queen of flowers,
And, from those faint Elysian bowers
Where thou, all-languorous, dost recline
In blushing loveliness divine,
Stretch forth thy rosy finger-tips
And touch my brow, or with thy lips
One nectarous kiss impress, and thrill
My throbbing spirit to thy will!
What rich unspeakable delights
Hast thou within thy summer nights!—
When fair Selene rules the sky
Deck'd in star-robes of majesty ;
When trees keep whispering in their sleep
Of lovers' secrets they would keep,
And in their dreams stretch amorous arms
To seize the passing zephyrs' charms ;
When diamonds sparkle in the grass,
Dropt from thy skirt as thou dost pass :
And silence, like a calming hand,
Lies softly on the slumbering land :
Then breathes a spirit on the air,
A subtle presence everywhere—
How palpable, and yet how rare !
    And the leaves shiver
      With a strange delight,
    And the moon-struck river
      Laughs silvery bright ;
    And the flowers are weeping
      Joy-tears of dew,
    And the birds from sleeping
      Are stirred anew ;
For Anthea, queen of flowers, is near,
And all is expectation here !

Celestial, thou canst well divine
What's in this longing heart of mine!
Wilt grant the wish which oft hath striven
For fitting utterance to heaven?
Here, on this flowery bank I lie—
Come, some ethereal touches try!
My heart, my thoughts, my will, are thine—
Exalt, with ecstasy divine,
In thine own secret of the flowers,
That now exert their mystic powers!
Though here, like us, they find their birth,
They speak a language not of earth;
This night, make thou their meaning plain,
Nor take perception back again!

Thou wavest thy hand across mine eyes—
In fainting ecstasy of sighs
I slip into the realm of dreams,
Where all that's mystery common seems,
Where vague perceptions of earth-sense
Take form and substance more intense
Than vain realities of earth,
Which have but seeming there, not birth.
Ha, charmer! what is this I feel—
What strange sensations o'er me steal!
I sink—I melt with sweet distress—
Immortal!—not too closely press
The gifts which now I sought from thee,
And knew not my enormity!
What universe of spirits bright
Throng round me, fluttering with delight—
Touch my fine senses, till they thrill
Responsive to their subtle will!
'Tis here, and there, and everywhere,
I see sprites beautiful and rare,
All working, sporting merrily,
And all in perfect harmony,

Who only can, in feeble way,
Express themselves to mortal clay—
Through twinkling dewdrop, sun, and shower,
Through form and fragrance of each flower,
Through tree, and grass, and purling stream,
Speak of a universe of dream,
A universe unseen, the true,
Whence springeth all that meets earth-view,
To draw men from their sense of earth,
And teach them of their nobler birth.
Here, clustering round, are forms of grace
Too fine for mortal hand to trace ;
Have pity on a mortal, pray,
Who would beside you ever stay,
To draw sustaining, quickening powers
From your dear blandishments, sweet flowers !—
One kiss—pass on—for at the morn
I wake to life and thought forlorn,
And must, ere then, in spirit see
Those of you that my favourites be !

CROCUS.

Tell me, pretty little fellow,
With the coat of golden yellow,
    What's your name, my merry sprite ?
" Simple mortal, lost in dreaming !
Don't you know me by my seeming,
    Don't you know the crocus bright ?

" 'Bye to thee ! the Spring is calling,
Birds are singing, waters falling,
    Buds are peeping timidly ;
Sister Snowdrop waits my coming,
Silent is the bees' glad humming
    Till the Crocus bright they see !"

SNOWDROP, PRIMROSE, AND MIGNONNETTE.

Maidens pale, maidens fair,
Maidens delicate and rare,
　Snowdrop and Primrose!
With another darling maid,
Mignonnette, demure and staid,
　Kiss your lover e'er he goes!

NARCISSUS.

Fairy with the pale, pure face
Form of symmetry and grace,
　Classic, tender Narcissus!
'Neath Sēlenē's silver beams
Tearfully thy beauty gleams,
　Supplicatingly for us!

Dost thou not, in fragrant prayer,
Sigh thy soul upon the air,
　Droop thy beauteous glistening head?
Have we not a finer sense
That must find some recompense
　For the love or beauty fled?

O my love, my pensive love,
Hearts on earth can soar above
　Sorrow, wrong, and thoughts of death,
When, with radiance pure and calm,
Thou dost gaze, or, like a balm,
　Breathest on us with thy breath!

WALLFLOWER.

Who is this in brown and gold,
With the mellow fragrance old?
　Favourite Wallflower—none but she!
Come along, my darling sprite,

Many a quaff of pure delight
Thou hast sure bestowed on me!

High on craggy, shaggy peaks,
Where the wild kae nesting seeks,
  Often hast thou beckoned me:
"Come up hither, till I give
Scent-thoughts that will ever live
  In thy heart and memory!"

In my heart and memory fine
Thou art there, sweet Wallflower, mine,
  And forever there shalt be;
Wave on wave of fragrant thought
Through my secret soul hath wrought
  Me a willing slave to thee!

ROSE.

Flower of flowers, my Rose, my own!
Thou and I are not unknown
  To each other, where we be;
Oft thy praises have I sung,
O'er thy fragrant petals hung,
  Mute with tearful ecstasy!

Love's own language pure thou art—
Fragrant passion at thy heart,
  Blushing beauty on thy face;
Lovers' pleadings ne'er shall fail
While thy fragrant thoughts prevail,—
  Let all words to thee give place!

What, only this one glimpse to me,
Fair Anthea, thy true devotee?
Come, sprites belovéd, ere I go,
One last fond kiss on me bestow—
Narcissus, Rose, and Mignonnette,

And modest Wallflower—sweet quartette!
Ah——! Heaven may boast of weaker bliss
Than concentrates in such a kiss!
Breathe on, sweet flowers, with airs divine,
And lead my heart to issues fine;
I know not all ye would express,
Yet love you more for this, not less,
And only long for finer powers
To feel your fragrant meaning, flowers!

————◦⋙◦——

REGARD ME NOT.

REGARD me not with measured love,
    And call it love: yon heaven
Is not more set the earth above
    Than love o'er love so given:
Regard me not with love at all,
If thou such weakness loving call.

To love, the heart—to thought, the head,
    Nor canst thou, loving, will;
When all thy powers of thought are dead,
    Sweet love shall move thee still:
Thou mayest long, devise, and choose—
When love commands, who may refuse?

Then, seek thou not, with thoughtful care,
    To regulate thy heart,
For love and thought can never pair,
    Or have an equal part:
But let full love control all thought,
And all thy thinking is as nought.

—◦⋙◦—

AFTER.

TO J. K.

COME, dear, and put your hand in mine,
　Without a single sound,
And turn to me that tearful face,
　Nor gaze so strange around.
What though our child is gone,
　And we are left to sigh?
'Tis we who mourn since we live on,
　But joy is theirs who die.

Come, look into my face, my dear,
　And see me smile to thee,
And in the confidence I show,
　Thou'lt find some sympathy.
Thou wilt not say that I
　Had less of love than thou,
Yet, since I know 'tis well with her,
　To what is well, I bow.

Fear not, my dear, who mournest now,
　There's joy in store for all,
There's not a flower but cries of love,
　Yet blooms that it may fall.
From Heaven, our darling came,
　To Heaven, to Heaven, she's gone—
'Tis but a memory, a name,
　That in our hearts lives on.

S T A R S.

O Stars, Stars ! silent, cold, and bright,
  Mysterious warders of the earth,
Deep slumbering through this summer night,
  With slumbering smiles of summer mirth :
Look down on earth with watchful gaze,
But mourners scorn your chilling rays.

How oft, how oft, unheedingly,
  Have ye heard mortal cry of pain,
When with heart-grief exceeding, we
  Have sought your sympathy in vain :
The burden of our earth-born grief,
Can never find in you relief.

But when we smile—aha, 'tis then,
  O winking sycophants ! that ye
Can to bright greeting smile again,
  With hateful, heartless mimicry !
Oh, rather cold and distant gaze,
Than shine with pale and mocking rays !

Shine o'er us, stars, of nobler sphere,
  With softer ray, with loving gleam,
Shine for our help, who wander here,
  Nor know reality from dream—
Shine on, shine on ! for soon your rays
Faint in the glorious morning's blaze !

———◦❈◦———

GAE AWA', GIN YE DAUR.

Gae awa', gin ye daur,
                    Ha, ha !
Gae awa', gin ye daur !
But, my lad, ye're owre leal,

An' I ken ye owre weel,
Sae, you needna think to steal
Frae your ain kind lass awa',
                    Ha, ha!
Frae your ain kind lass awa'!

Here's my airms ootstretcht to thee,
                    Ha, ha!
Here's my airms ootstretcht to thee!
Here's my mou', that ye ca' bonnie—
Come an' pree it, dearest Johnnie,
For I lo'e ye mair than ony,
An' ye needna gae awa,'
                    Ha, ha!
An' ye needna gae awa'!

Weel I wat hoo ye wad feel,
                    Ha, ha!
Weel I wat hoo ye wad feel!
It's frae dawnin' o' the licht
I'd be never oot your sicht,
An' ye'd dream o' nocht at nicht
But your lassie faur awa',
                    Ha, ha!
But your lassie faur awa'!

Oh, ye needna say ye'll dae't,
                    Ha, ha!
Oh, ye needna say ye'll dae't!
Here, puir laddie, tak' my haun',
Dinna glowerin', switherin' staun'—
Ye maun bide whan I comman',
An' ye couldna gae awa',
                    Ha, ha!
Could ye—*could* ye gae awa'?

SCOTLAND'S HEROES.

To you, brave warriors of our land,
This offering of my heart and hand !
To Wallace, Bruce, and noble host
Of fearless men, their country's boast,
Their country's honour and its pride,
Whom there is none to place beside,
Save he, perchance, whose thrilling lyre
Could e'en inspire a patriot's fire ;
To you who fought and nobly fell,
Unconquered and unconquerable,
Till men who live might long to die,
To live as you, eternally
Enshrined within our grateful love,
As sacred as yon heaven above !
O Wallace, Bruce ! Down through the mist
Of gathering years, whose suns have kiss'd
Your hills so oft with summer glow,
Or winters garbed in glistening snow,
And spread o'er plains on which you fought,
And with your blood our freedom bought,
Sweet flowers of spring, from that red rain,
To bloom, to die, and bloom again,
Five hundred times, in peaceful round,
All undisturbed by war's dread sound—
Down through the vista of the years
That gleams eniris'd by our tears,
From these weak days of feeble strife—
Faint radiations of that life
Of simple faith and confidence
Of which your acts gave evidence—
We stretch out loving hands, O ye
Who wrought not for our sympathy !
Our Heroes ! when to you we turn,
What aspirations in us burn !
What throbbings of the head and heart,

What pulsings through our being dart—
What nervous clutchings of the hand
That would have drawn at your command,
And, swinging sword of battle high,
Rushed on to conquer or to die!
What fierce endeavours in us stir
To break the bands of gossamer
That bind our feeble limbs of clay—
Degenerate of a later day!

If men there be as ye—'tis well :
Let future bards their virtues tell !
But he alone the hero true
Who finds his noble work to do,
Nor seeks reward or recompense
From feeble man's incompetence,
But in himself, and in his deeds,
Finds all the strengthening which he needs.
Shades of my Heroes, dear and brave !
Not too familiarly I wave
A greeting, less in words than tears
That have no meaning that appears.
There's not a sprig of fragrant heath
But speaks to me a hero's death ;
There's not a hill that strikes the sky,
Or river gliding gently by,
A simple bluebell by the way,
But speak of things far more than they—
But seem, in language loud and clear,
To fill my grateful eye and ear—
" From patriots' love, from patriots' blood,
We stand, we spring, we have our flood ! "

O love, love, love—so manifold !
In these, our noble men of old,
Who scorned all life that they might give
To us the liberty to live,
We see the same fond power command

Which moves the gentle heart and hand
In peaceful bye-ways of our life,
Afar from turbulent war or strife ;
The same fine influence of our land
Of wood, and stream, and mountain grand,
Of fragrant heath and rugged glen—
Inspiring and ennobling men
Even in these days, as days of yore,
Though now perchance, to fight no more
To keep thee from invading foe,
Or tyrants' swarming hosts o'erthrow :
We recognise thee, love, and own
From thee all preciousness alone !
Conform thy children weak, and raise,
Till we shall live what now we praise !

HAST THOU.

HAST thou, indeed, surprise
　　Within thy heart,
And grieving in thine eyes,
　　That we must part ?
Dost thou, O Sweet, presume
　　Our borrowed love,　　　　　.
That lit life's wildering gloom,
　　Mounts earth above ?
Aha, my dear, my only dear—
There is no lasting loving here.

We may believe, indeed,
　　This love is ours,
And, in our longing need,
　　Yield to love's powers.
Our need is great, my dear,
　　Our need is strong,
But love, to mortals here,
　　Doth not belong :
Some finer sphere, some purer race,
Love fitly may illume and grace.

F I N I S.

I SEE, I see, the closing page
  Of thee, my book, has come :
How oft, perchance, had I been sage,
  Hadst thou been only dumb ! ✝ ·

Yet, though recorded in each line
  The feelings of the hour,
The Poet's faith and hopes divine,
  His feebleness or power,—

This heart of mine will ne'er regret
  A thousand throbs and sighs,
And secret tears that oft have wet
  A Poet's longing eyes.

Within my heart of hearts I feel
  Each labouring human breast
A precious beauty doth conceal
  That is not oft confess'd ;

And he who utters from his own,
  Doth speak for other hearts :
Not for his own sweet ease alone
  An utterance Heaven imparts.

If one faint gleam, one feeble spark
  Of Heavenly flame be mine,
To beckon upward, through the dark—
  I never can repine.

Not with a careless hand I lay
  Thee silently aside ;
Thy volume is complete to-day,
  Though nought may long abide.

And if 'tis so, I heed it not—
  So short, so trifling, life ;
It comes, it goes, it is forgot,
  With all its dreamy strife.